TWISTED THORNS

BOOK ONE OF THE CALDER DUET

✦

ALEXIS NIGHT

For those who are finding themselves again.

If everything around seems dark, look again, you may be the light.

-Rumi

Copyright © 2024 by Alexis Night

All rights reserved.

No part of this book may be reproduced in any form or by any electronic or mechanical means, including information storage and retrieval systems, without written permission from the author, except for the use of brief quotations in a book review. For permission requests, contact Alexis Night.

The story, all names, characters, and incidents portrayed in this production are fictious. No identification with actual persons (living or deceased), places, buildings, and products is intended or should be inferred.

Paperback: 979-8-3245571-6-4

Book Cover and Interior Illustrations by Alexis Night

Editing and proofreading by S. Moore

First edtion 2024

Author Note

Please know your boundaries. Twisted Thorns is an adult romance novel with dark themes, including mention of violence, memories of a car accident, abduction, trafficking, and torture. This is an open-door romance and contains consensual explicit sexual scenes with some elements of BDSM, including bondage and dominance. Your mental health matters.

Pronounciation Guide

Avalina Hartwell
ava-lina heart-well

Kieran Calder
keer-an kAHl-der

Cruinniuc
kren-you

Macha
makh-uh

Niamh
neeve

Oisín
osh-een

Sadhbh
sigh-ve

Serch Bythol
serk beeth-ohl

Tír na n-Óg
teer-nah-nOHg

Chapter 1

Avalina

The laughter of my friends echo in the bustling coffee shop, a sound that once brought me joy but now caused a dull ache in my chest. Sitting in an overstuffed chair, I glance around at the exposed brick walls and the Edison lanterns that hang from the ceilings. This place may look cozy, with its mindfully curated nooks and crannies through artfully placed furniture, but a deeper look reveals everything here is expensive. Kingdale's art gallery curated the artwork along the walls. The counters are sleek, dark marble, where you can get a designer cupcake with edible gold on it. And most of the customers are wearing luxury designer clothes, with a few couture standouts.

My hands run along the dark green velvet plush under my fingers. I'm trying to keep up with my friends' conversation about work, relationships, and the latest gossip, the latter of which Amanda is presently filling Claire and me in on. But when the topic veers towards something I can't remember, I'm overwhelmed with feeling like an outsider wearing a mask.

"Did you hear about Jessica's engagement? She's getting married in Bali next year," Amanda says, sipping on her iced latte and brushing her chestnut hair behind her.

"Wow, that'll be incredible," I reply, feigning enthusiasm as I pick at the foam on my cappuccino, battling the panic that inevitably reigns its head in moments like this. This is when I feel the most guilt for not being able to remember. I want to be happy for Jessica, but I don't remember her or her boyfriend-now-fiancé.

Can you even be friends with someone you can't remember? My heart says no, but then I recall how Jessica was by my side at the hospital. All my friends were there, bringing me delicious foods and glossy magazines, showing me pictures and video of the time before the accident that I couldn't recall.

So now I feel like I owe it to my friends to play pretend, even if it feels like I'm swallowing rocks instead of my feelings. They've done so much for me over the past few months. Who am I to tell them it's not enough? One day I'm afraid the feelings I've been shoving down will break through the fragile facade I've built since the day I woke up in the hospital.

"I know, I'm so excited! And you know we'll all be bridesmaids." Amanda squeals. Apparently, she and Jessica have already been talking about wedding colors and floral arrangements, which brings joy to Amanda's event planning heart. Her eyes sparkle as she talks about the designer dresses she suggested to Jessica.

I swallow against the alarm crawling up my throat, letting my mind drift back to the serenity of the woods behind my apartment, the comforting embrace of nature that I've craved since the accident. I feel so out of place here, pretending to be interested in the same things as my friends to fit in. Pretending to remember.

While the girls around me chat about wedding cake flavors, I'm daydreaming about the way the violet ironweed shines in the early morning light, a memory that soothes my racing pulse. I can almost see the vibrant purple petals of the ironweed dancing gracefully in the gentle breeze, glistening with dewdrops in the golden sunlight.

"Earth to Avie. You there?" Claire asks, snapping me out of my thoughts. "We were talking about planning a girls' trip to Miami."

"Sorry, I just... I'm not sure if that's really my thing anymore." I hesitate, knowing my words will only widen the distance between us. "Everything feels so different now."

"Come on, Avie! You used to love our trips!" Amanda insists, her heart-shaped face filled with confusion as she looked at me.

Claire jumps in before I can respond. "And I bet she'll love this one! Right, Avie?"

"Of course, I'm sure I will." My fingers nervously toy with my necklace, guilt thrumming through me like the plucked strings of a guitar. I can't decide between going along with the plan like I suspect old Avalina would do, or admitting that I had no memory of our getaways and don't want to take a trip.

Claire is always trying to play peacemaker these days between me and Amanda. I understand Amanda's frustration with my lack of memories. I met her in the five years currently missing from my mind, so to her we are friends, but I still view her as a stranger.

Some days, the unspoken friction feels like a web I can't unravel, and all my attempts just have me more tangled in the threads that used to hold our friendship together.

"Oh! I almost forgot!" Amanda's face lit up as she leaned across the table. "There's a new nightclub opening up next week. We should go. Maybe we can find someone for Avie," she chuckles as her shoulder bumps into mine. "You haven't dated anyone since Jake and that was, what, two years ago?"

I smile and try to play along, but deep inside, my stomach is twisting up in knots. I don't even remember who Jake is. Maybe I used to have a better poker face, but Amanda sees right through me.

"You don't want to go?" Amanda pouts. "It's no fun if we all don't go."

I struggle to find the right words. To explain that my life feels like an old sweater. Something loved, but full of holes and threadbare. It doesn't quite fit me anymore. "Things have changed ever since the accident, and I guess that used to be something I'd like, but now I'm not so sure."

"But we always go together." Amanda begins, and the dam is bursting before I even have time to register my fists are clinching and anger is bubbling in my veins.

"I don't want to go!" I yell, my skin suddenly hot and tight, and I'm not sure if it's from my anger or embarrassment.

Silence falls over the table, and I can feel the confusion settling in like fog on a lake. The gap between my friends and I feel like an abyss, filled with all the memories we share I can no longer access. Panic swoops in at the thought of disappointing my friends, taking my ability to think along with it. My thoughts scatter like shards of glass, leaving me grasping for words to explain what I mean.

"I need some air," I murmur, excusing myself from the table as I rush outside, eager to escape the suffocating silence after my declaration. But I know I can't escape it for long. I can't take back the words I said. Not when it means speaking up for the first time in months.

The tinkling bell of the coffee shop door has me turning to see my best friend walking my way. "We're just worried about you, Avalina. We want you to be happy," Claire says as she approaches my side. I look into her furrowed blue eyes, seeing the concern etched in the crinkled corners.

"I know you do, and I appreciate it. But I'm not the same person I was before the accident. Five years of memories are gone. Five years of myself are gone. I need to figure out who I am now, even if it means leaving some things behind."

"Even us?" she asks, her voice wavering, and she wraps her arms around herself against the chilly autumn air.

"No, of course not," I reassure her. "But our friendship might change, and we'll have to navigate that together. It's hard watching you talk about things that I can't remember. Things that I may never remember."

Claire sighs, and her forehead burrows in sadness, but I know she understands me.

Of all my friends, Claire is the only one I remember. She's my childhood best friend, and I've been following her infectious smile and carefree spirit into trouble since we were both toddlers.

Before the accident, I worked with Claire at the art gallery. It seems like we've done everything together in life, including going to the same college and getting art history degrees.

Apparently, college is where we met Amanda and Jessica, who both studied fashion design.

Claire has been my lifeline through these interactions with Amanda and Jessica, who I only remember through stories I'm told. But in moments like this, Claire feels further apart than ever.

In a lot of ways, Claire feels like the opposite of me now - her with her light blonde hair and baby blue eyes, always cheerful and outgoing. Meanwhile, I feel like a wallflower. I wonder if I felt like this before the accident. I wonder if I just hid my feelings then better than I do now.

"Okay," Claire says gently, pulling me into a hug. "Just promise you won't totally disappear on us."

"I promise." I hug her back, grateful for her understanding but knowing that my journey to rediscover myself will be a solitary one. After all, I'm the only one who can't remember the past five years. Even though my friends have shown me pictures and videos, it still doesn't piece together the gaps in my mind.

Everyone else may not want to admit it, but having that chunk of time lost did more than make it impossible to remember things. It changed who I am. From what I can piece together, I don't have the same interest as I did before the accident, and it's driving a wedge between who I am and who everyone expects me to be.

Pulling my phone from my pocket, I type out a text to the girls letting them know I'm headed home, walking to my car as I send it. I know it's cowardly, but I just don't have it in me to face their disappointment again. I want to be the Avalina they remember, but I just don't know who that is anymore.

The drive home is a blur, as my warring emotions have me on autopilot during the short drive to the edge of town where my apartment is. Parking my car in its numbered spot, I look up at the building my apartment is in. The lower half of the building is encased in red brick, while the second and third floors are accented with siding in cream and robin egg blue as you go up. Balconies peek out from various apartments, with large windows overlooking the manicured walking trails and playgrounds. Most would say these luxury apartments are prized for their designer kitchens and bathrooms, or the resort-style pool. I just wanted my apartment to be on the first floor, as close to the forest behind the complex as possible.

I visit the woods almost daily now, and a part of me wants to visit them now, but the darkening gray sky promises rain. Grabbing my purse, I slide out of my car and drag myself towards my door, sighing as I step into the welcoming space, breathing in the scent of jasmine and sandalwood. All I want to do is relax, but my muscles feel tense, like they're bracing for the next disaster. Now that the adrenaline has worn off, I can feel my mind slipping into old habits, wanting to berate myself for not being able to go along with what my friends want.

I step into my kitchen to make some tea when a knock sounds at my door. Opening it, I find the familiar face of my younger sister, Iris.

Iris and I look similar, both with copper colored hair and green eyes, but Iris shines with an optimism that lights up any room.

A smile spread across her face as she catches sight of me, her hair cut in a pixie cut that frames her delicate features.

"Hey, Avie," she greets me, stepping inside and enveloping me in a hug. "How are you holding up?"

"Surviving," I sigh, feeling the weight of my recent conversation with Claire. I have a hunch that conversation is why Iris is here, but I decide to wait it out, at least for now. "I was just going to make some tea. Do you want some?"

Iris makes a shooing motion, moving me away from the kitchen and into the small living room. "You sit down. I'll make the tea."

I know my sister is up to something, but I let her take over as a mother hen, curling up on the couch under my favorite purple throw. Being only a couple of years younger than me, Iris and I share a lot of the same friends, something that annoyed me when we were younger, but now I'm grateful for. Iris helps fill in the gaps in my memory and often makes suggestions for how I can try to reconnect with my friends again. While our parents love us, they are out of town a lot, going on elaborate vacations now that they are retired. Without them around recently, Iris has taken on the role of big sister and mother hen all in one.

Conan, my brown tabby cat, meows at me before he leaps up and begins kneading the soft blanket. Petting Conan, I look around the small space. It isn't much, but it's all mine and that's what matters to me. It's a one-bedroom apartment with a kitchen just big enough to cook in that opens to the living area. Everything is light wood and soft pillows and blankets, all in the muted hues of a spring sunrise. Pale sky blue walls are accented with buttery lace curtains, a lilac knitted throw tossed over a cream couch dotted with creamsicle and rose floral pillows.

But the best part? The floor to ceiling bookshelves I had installed on the longest wall in the living room, overflowing with novels. A stack of books on Celtic mythology and fables sits on the coffee table, dried flowers and leaves acting as bookmarks.

I watch my sister boil water and rummage around my tea cabinet, pulling down my favorite mug. "Let me guess, Claire called you?"

"Listen," she says, pulling away from her task, her eyes shining with determination. "I've been thinking about how we can help you reconnect with the girls. What if we plan a getaway? Just us and them, spending some quality time together."

I inwardly groan. I wasn't ready to have this conversation. Perhaps I wouldn't ever be ready to have this conversation. I feel like a broken doll everyone is trying to mend. I pick at the threads of the blanket, my hands eager to do *something*.

"Maybe," I hesitate, the thought of facing my friends' expectations again makes my stomach churn.

But I know that Iris only has my best interests at heart, and the idea of escaping the city for a while holds a certain appeal. And Iris has been my rock since the accident, helping me feel comfortable being just where I am at.

"I think it will be good for you, Avie." she insists, bringing over two steaming mugs of tea. "Some time away from all the things that remind you of the accident. Think of it like a fresh start with your friends."

"Okay," I reluctantly agree, knowing that if anyone could help me bridge the gap between my old life and my new reality, it's Iris. While I appreciate her help, I know I'll have to fly on my own soon.

Chapter 2

Avalina

Last night was another sleepless night, but this time, instead of nightmares, it was my guilt plaguing me. Rubbing my eyes, I try to wipe the exhaustion away, along with my doubt. Was I too harsh with Amanda? She was trying to be a good friend and include me. Maybe I was just getting in my own way.

Throwing on some leggings and an oversized sweater, I tie up my sneakers and make my way to the woods behind my apartment building, pulling up my hair in a low ponytail as I walk.

Walking through the woods has become a sacred ritual for me, a reprieve from the darkness that haunts my sleepless nights. Ever since the car accident three months ago, nightmares plagued my sleep, leaving me breathless and drenched in sweat. Images of twisted metal and shattered glass startle me wide awake, but the memories remain elusive, slipping through my fingers like sand.

At the edge of the woods, my eyes search the horizon while my copper hair dances around my shoulders, tickled by the breeze. Closing my eyes, I take a deep breath in, the rich scent of the loamy earth enveloping me. The beauty surrounding me wraps me in a cocoon, letting me just *be*.

If there's one thing I've come to appreciate since the accident, it's moments like this embraced by stillness and peace.

The damp soil falls beneath my shoes as I trek further through the woods, softened by yesterday evening's rain, a sign we're moving away from the hot days of summer into the crisp embrace of fall.

The trees, with their ancient wisdom, seem to whisper reassurances as I pass them by. They don't care about the gaps in my memories or the questions that linger unanswered. They just stand tall, inviting me to find peace amongst their roots. These elder sentinels help me feel not so alone in a world where I feel so out of place.

As I wander deeper into the woods, I let my thoughts drift back to the event that changed my life forever. Here, surrounded by the trees, I can let everything go and forget the nagging feeling that I'm missing more than just memories.

The first few days in the hospital were a blur, filled with tests and doctors and worried faces. I was bruised and scratched all over, a map of disaster made flesh, with a broken leg, fractured ribs, and a concussion. The latter of which was the most worrisome, as some faces of my visitors were like strangers to me.

The doctors assured my parents and sister that it was temporary, and once the swelling went down, my memories would clear. But days soon turned into weeks, and the only thing that became clear was that some memories were gone.

It was like someone came in and took out a chunk of time, the past five years, to be exact. Five years of old faces that were now new to me. Of childhood friends who had weddings and children I knew nothing about.

A handful of years doesn't seem long until it's ripped from your grasp, the only remaining thread a frayed ribbon of dark dreams that leaves a stain of uncertainty on everything it touches.

I was a lone boat in the storm, trapped by the waves of memories I couldn't overcome. It was a constant struggle to accept the person I had become, a stranger even to myself. I couldn't recall the details of the past five years, years that contained memories that had shaped me, and it left a void that gnawed at my soul.

"Focus on what you have now," my therapist had advised me at our last appointment. "It's okay to mourn the person you were, but don't let it consume you."

Easier said than done. I wasn't sure who I was now.

While my friends and family had regarded my missing memories with understanding at first, I had the sense that an undercurrent of resentment had been building in some of my friends. My lack of memory was a thorn in their side that they just couldn't dislodge.

I felt like I didn't fit in, no matter how hard I tried, and I was certain it was because of those years lost in the recesses of my mind. I was desperate to remember, clinging to the hope that once my memories returned, everything would feel normal again.

The breeze brushed against my skin, offering a gentle caress as though to remind me that I too could find freedom in the present moment.

If only I knew how.

The sound of birdsong pulls me from my reverie, and I look up to watch a pair of finches flit between the branches overhead. I envy their freedom, their ability to spread their wings and take flight, leaving their troubles behind.

The forest is alive with energy, and I can't help but feel a sense of belonging here, among the trees and the creatures who call this place home.

It's a stark contrast to the life outside of these trees, where I feel like an outsider in my own existence. In the woods, I don't need to remember that party last summer or what Halloween costume I wore three years ago that everyone thought was hilarious.

I am enough, just as I am now.

"Another night filled with terrors," I whisper to myself, frustrated by the endless chasm between my past and present. "Why can't I remember?"

Despite the comfort I find in these woods, there is a part of me that longs to reclaim the memories that were stolen by that fateful day.

Each day, as I wander beneath these branches, I search for clues to my past, piecing together fragments of what was lost.

Through pictures and video, stories, and scrapbooks, I had glimpsed the past five years: a young woman fresh out of college, living in a small apartment in the town she grew up in. I had a large group of friends and seemed to keep up with the designer trends and go to parties, working with my best friend at a local art gallery.

Money was power in my world, but none of that interested me now. All of it felt strange, like I was looking at someone else's life. I felt like there had to be something missing, some key memory that was keeping me from feeling at home as myself.

"Maybe today will be different," I tell myself, daring to hope. "Embrace the now, Avalina."

Making my way to my treasured spot beneath a towering, time-worn oak tree, I settle myself down, feeling the rough, knotted roots underneath my legs and the comforting embrace of the curved bark against my back. This oak is off to the side of the meandering path, and its large canopy provides the perfect shelter from the heat of the sun. I let my eyes flutter closed as I breathe deeply, the sounds and fragrance of the woods comforting me. Alarm peels through me as I get a whiff of smoke, and my eyes shoot open, frantically glancing around me. Nothing seems amiss as I look around. All I see is the dappled sunlight glancing off the forest ferns, the small flowers of white snakeroot peeking in between their leaves.

Rifling in my backpack, I search until I find my treasure—the latest book I borrowed from the library. It contains ancient myths and fables from Ireland, a world I've never seen but call to me all the same. I like to get lost in the words I find on the pages to escape my reality for a little while, and something about the idea of green, rolling hills with stories of fae and swans calls to me.

Nature, books, and the library. Those were the things my life centered on now. They soothed the static that buzzed in my mind most days. The library, especially, with its familiar scents of ink and aged paper, enveloped me like a warm embrace. The soft murmur of pages turning and the distant echo of footsteps on polished floors created a symphony of knowledge, a song that spoke to the deepest parts of my soul.

I return my attention to my book, intent on letting my mind escape from the toil of trying to figure it all out, at least for a moment. I know the answers are there, but they often feel like they are just out of reach. A nightmare of running from a monster, but never getting closer to the safety of home.

Everyone keeps telling me I just need more time, that with it my memories will come back, but it has been months, and no new memories have emerged since the accident. We don't even know what caused the accident. I desperately want to move forward and put the accident behind me. But I'm not sure how to do that when it haunts my days and nights, a specter I can never outrun.

Chapter 3

Kieran

I release my tight grip on the heavy glass of whiskey as I set it back down on the table, bruised knuckles aching with the effort. Shifting in my seat, I tugged my sleeve down to hide the dried blood on my arm. I must have missed it in my time in the washroom on my way here. The bar is dimly lit, the only source of light coming from the flickering lights hanging above. The air is thick with the smell of smoke and alcohol, a familiar scent that I've grown accustomed to over the years. I take a deep breath, inhaling the sharp scent of whiskey mixed with the faint aroma of tobacco.

Glancing around the bar, I take in the other patrons. A group of men in designer suits take up an entire corner, their voices rising with each swig of their beers. A lone woman sits at the bar, nursing a glass of wine, her eyes darting anxiously around the room. And then there's me, sitting alone at a small booth in the corner, nursing my whiskey and trying to drown out the chaos of the world outside.

But even in the darkness and solitude of this bar, I can't escape the memories that haunt me. It isn't the lives I've taken to protect what's ours that keep me away at night. It's how I don't mind doing it.

I take another sip of my whiskey, letting the burn of the alcohol distract me from my thoughts. But it's only temporary. Soon enough, I'll have to face my demons once again. But for now, I'll sit here and drown them out, one glass at a time.

I look up to see my brother Liam settling down in the booth across from me. The table creaks with age as he leans across and tosses back the rest of my whiskey.

I can't help but notice the shadows under his eyes as he pushes his dark hair out of his face. "Long day?" I ask.

His shoulders shrug with resignation, and he glances around. "You know how it is."

Unfortunately, I do. He doesn't sleep well and spends most of his days knocking back alcohol and pushing his body beyond what it can take. But I say nothing. I have said it all before.

For everyone else, Liam is the charmer, the smooth talker. His dark, shaggy hair and baby blue eyes get him into as much trouble as it gets him out of. With me, he lets his guard down. Only I see the demons haunting him.

My own demons are haunting me tonight as well. The bells on the door chime, announcing more patrons have arrived. My gaze falls upon Avalina Hartwell, her long copper hair cascading down her back like a waterfall. Her outfit, a plain white t-shirt and ripped jeans, stands out among the designer dresses and tailored suits of the other guests. She looks like a wildflower in a field of perfectly manicured roses. She just doesn't fit in. As much as everyone has seemed to try to reel her back in, to bring her back to the fold, she just stands out more. I watch her from across the room, unable to tear my eyes away.

"Kieran, are you even listening?" Liam's voice breaks through my reverie, forcing me to turn my attention back to him. "You seem distracted." Turning on his charm, he gives me a look and leans towards me, tattooed hands splayed across the table. "Who is it?" He glances over at the bar.

"Oh, fuck off," I murmur, my gaze flickering back to Avalina for a moment before I force it away. "There's just a lot on my mind. Plus, we're waiting for Finn. We don't have time to get into this."

Leaning back, he rests his hands behind his head in a way that lets me know he doesn't believe the lie, but he'll let it slide, anyway.

"Whatever you say, big bro."

Rolling my shoulders, I attempt to loosen some of the tension that has gathered there, no doubt from my conversation earlier that led to my bruised knuckles.

A commotion near Avalina interrupts my thoughts; a man raises his voice, his words slurred with drink, and though she tries to defuse the situation with her characteristic poise, I can see the unease flicker across her face like a shadow. Instantly, my instincts are on high alert, the desire to protect her surging through me like the rising tide.

"Excuse me, I need another drink," I say to Liam, my voice tight as I stride towards Avalina, determined to shield her from harm. As I approach, the man stumbles away from her, muttering under his breath, and I can feel the tension in my chest ease only slightly at the sight of her, safe and unharmed.

"Are you all right?" I ask, my concern for her eclipsing my own preoccupations.

"Thank you," she whispers, her green eyes capturing mine as she smiles. "I'm fine, really."

"Good," I reply, unable to keep the relief from my voice as I watch her return to her friends. With every step she takes, I want nothing more than to go with her and keep her safe.

I order a couple more drinks at the bar before heading back to Liam, who is smirking at me as I hand him his whiskey. "You can't stop every drunken fool in here from being an ass, you know."

"Perhaps not," I concede, though I know that won't stop me from trying.

"What's with you playing knight in shining armor, anyway?" Liam quirks an eyebrow at me.

"I've had enough fights for one night, that's all," I reply as I sink back into the booth. Liam glances at my knuckles scattered with blues and purples but says nothing.

We were born into this family and bound to it by not only the blood coursing through our veins, but the ones in our nightmares as well. I've learned it's best to not dwell and just focus on the task at hand. I'm about to do just that when I hear Avalina's laugh from across the room, shifting my thoughts entirely.

Avalina doesn't remember me, but I remember her. The secret meetings, longing glances, and nights spent together, separating before dawn broke through the clouds. Even then, Avalina was feeling torn between duty and desire. Between being the socialite that everyone around her expected her to be and being her own person, free to make her own choices without feeling the need to fit in.

I understood her frustrations and feeling caught in a web of your own making. I felt the same between the family business and being my own man. We both were caught in the trap of expectations and found solace in each other.

But we were a secret. We met by chance. And now she doesn't remember me and our nights together, what we shared. But I'm watching her blossom and I fear that to be in her life again will only bring her back to where she doesn't want to be, that I'd drag her back into the darkness. My darkness.

My mind snags on a memory, my hand wrapped around Avalina's throat as she arched and writhed under me. Never would I have imagined that this pretty socialite was such a pretty submissive.

Fuck.

I pick up my whiskey again, downing the rest of the glass in one burning gulp. I shook my head like I was trying to shake these memories loose that were plaguing me. As much as I cared for Avalina, I would not bring her back to a place she didn't want to be.

She belonged in a world different from this one, one that she could be herself in and shine. I would only doom her to the shadows.

The server drops more whiskey off at our table and just in time, as the door opens to reveal the reason Liam and I are here to begin with.

Finnegan O'Neil barely lets his steel-gray eyes scan the room before he's making his way to us, his purposeful stride eating up the distance. He is a mountain of a man, all broad shoulders and thick arms, his dark red hair matching his beard.

Anyone else would bristle at the fact that Liam and I are sitting across from each other, which leaves Finn with a choice of which enemy he is going to sit next to. I inwardly smile as he slides in next to Liam. Finn has always had a good instinct about where the danger truly lies.

Leaning back, I quickly note the way Finn's weight is shifted to one side, no doubt because of the gun he has hidden. We're all armed right now, so I don't really care. Liam breaks the silence with one of his charming smiles. "How's Sloane doing?"

Finn's red eyebrows arch as he studies my brother before giving him the information he wants about his sister. "She's bored. She would rather be here at this meeting with us than sitting in her room staring at a boat moving across the ocean."

"She should just leave. Stop letting Sean keep her locked away like some princess."

I eye my brother. "That's the whole point, Liam. Sloane plays her part, so we have more inside intel. It's how we'll take Sean and his operation down."

Finn's father Sean is the head of the O'Neil family, and he is clutching to that role with an iron fist. Sean keeps telling Finn that he'll pass the job onto him soon, but it's been years now with no changing of the guard.

Rolling his eyes, Liam huffs and sips the whiskey I brought him.

Finn just laughs and punches my brother in the shoulder. "When are you going to admit you're hopelessly in love with my sister?"

"When she admits I exist beyond whenever she calls me."

"She just knows you're a good little puppy. You come when she calls."

"This puppy is about to bite your ass," Liam says as his eyes narrow.

"Can we get back to the topic, please?" I sigh, watching the two bicker.

Turning back to me, Finn says, "Jimmy recently mentioned to me he thought my father should step down soon, that it's best to retire in your prime so you don't get taken out back and shot like a dog."

I interrupt Finn. "But I thought Jimmy was one of Sean's loyal cronies?"

Finn nods. "So did I, but I guess things are changing."

"That or it's a test." Liam pipes in.

"Either way, I don't see it happening," Finn continues, "even if it did, we all know Slone should get the honors, not me. She's the eldest."

I snort. "We all know how Sean feels about women."

"Yeah, the only places they're acceptable are the kitchen or the bedroom." Liam chimes in.

"He's a fucking asshole," Finn replies before gesturing the server over to order a beer.

"Are we any closer with the intel about the shipment Sean's expecting?" I ask.

"Yeah, Sloane says it will be here in a few days." Finn says as he passes an envelope across the table to me.

I flip through the contents. "We still don't know what it is, though."

"Knowing my father, it's probably guns."

"Either way, the plan is still on. We interrupt the shipment and derail Sean's plans, whatever they are."

"And hopefully, cutting off the flow of money he is expecting."

"We know he won't stop, though. He'll just find another way to come by more power, no matter how dirty it is."

"That's why we have to force him out, so we can clean up the O'Neils like we cleaned up the Calders once our father passed away."

For someone like Sean, morals and a code don't apply if money and power are to me made. Drugs, trafficking, murder-for-hire, Sean will take it all.

Between me, Finn, Liam, and Sloane, we've been keeping tabs on Sean and trying to undermine his attempts to extend his reach, including cutting off his deals with sex traffickers and drug pushers.

"How'd the meeting with Rocco go?" Finn asks, his gaze sliding over to me, glancing at the fresh gashes on my fingers.

"Rocco and I had a nice little chat about attempting to exhort his staff with illegally taken photos and video for extra 'favors', I grumble, tossing back the rest of my drink.

"I still don't know why you didn't let me take care of Rocco," Liam says.

"Aw, is the little puppy feeling ignored?" Finn jokes. "You know how your brother is," he continues, "he needs to beat someone up now and then."

As our business winds down, Finn excuses himself and Liam moves to the bar to catch the attention of a redhead sitting there. So, I'm left alone and, of course, my mind and gaze drifts to Avalina.

I glance down at my almost empty glass of whiskey and contemplate ordering another, but no matter how drunk I get, I'll never erase the image of her from my mind.

Without something else to occupy it, my thoughts automatically drift to my last night with Avalina. The last time she remembered me.

Immediately, my senses are full of her. The silk of her hair wrapped around my hand, the smell of her skin, jasmine and sandalwood, the sound of her moans as I moved inside of her. I tossed the whiskey back, gritting my teeth against the fire. For a split second, the burn in my throat almost erased the burn in my heart.

Chapter 4

Avalina

Conan stretches out in front of me on my couch, swishing his striped tail to grab my attention. Running my hand along his soft fur, I smile as the gentle rumble of purring began. It is a pleasant distraction from the back-and-forth banter that is going on between Claire and Iris in my living room.

After Iris recently decided that a girls' weekend was what I needed to feel like myself and reconnect with my friends again, she roped in Claire to do the heavy lifting.

Iris is seemingly allergic to planning, while Claire has her entire life mapped out. But despite their differences, I know they'll come up with something special for the weekend ahead.

Even if I'm not completely sold on the idea of this trip, watching Iris and Claire work together to create a vacation everyone gets something out of is amusing.

I glance up to see Claire pulling out her phone. "Fine, we'll make a list."

"A list, really, Claire?" Iris groaned.

I held back a laugh. This was one reason I loved Claire. She has an enormous love of lists.

"Well, Amanda wants to go shopping. Jessica wants a spa day. You want a night out. Avalina wants books, and I want a museum. You try planning all of that without a list," Claire frowns, exasperation punctuating her words.

It doesn't really matter to me. I don't even want to get away. I just want answers.

Shaking off my wandering thoughts, I turn my attention back to Iris and Claire, laughing as I realize my best friend's single list has turned into multiple lists strewn about over my living room floor like confetti.

Claire's focus shifts from her colored-coded lists to me at my laugh. The gleam in her eye spells trouble.

"So, what was with Kieran Calder coming to your rescue at the bar the other night?" she asks as she begins sorting the paper into piles.

"I have no idea. I've never met him before," I begin, but then pause. "Wait, have I met him before?" My voice is rising with panic that yet another forgotten memory is getting in my way.

"No, no, none of us have met him." Iris jumps in, always ready to soothe my dread at a moment's notice.

"Yeah, you know how mysterious the Calder family is. No one ever gets close to them." Claire says.

I do remember that from before the accident. The influential Calder family rules over everything and everyone in Kingsdale. If you want to stay in the Calder's good graces, you play by their rules.

It was just that Kieran Calder kept popping into my head since that night at the bar when he came over after that drunk hit on me. The sight of his dark eyes lit a spark of recognition in me, but I'm not sure why.

I had only seen him a few times since my accident, all in public places around town, but every time I knew he was there before I saw him. It felt like there was a tether linking us together, a mental knot I keep trying to unravel.

Claire and Iris continue swapping getaway ideas, bouncing ideas off each other. I move Conan off my lap, stretching as I stand. "I'm going to make us some tea. Any requests?"

"Something with caffeine." Iris groans.

Chuckling, I make my way to my kitchen, putting the water on to boil and grabbing tea cups down from the cabinets. By the time I make my way back over to the girls, Claire beams up at me, handing me a piece of paper with what looks to be a list.

"What's this?" I ask.

"Our plan! I'm going to text it to the others."

In the end, we don't go far. We escape Kingsdale to go to the nearby Big Apple for some retail therapy. Kingsdale has plenty of shopping, but it is nothing like New York City.

The bright fluorescent lights of the boutique stores Amanda insists we stop at are blinding, and the endless rows of stores seem to stretch on forever. After hours of standing and walking, my feet are throbbing, and the weight of the bags in my hand is becoming unbearable. The girls walk ahead of me, their gazes scanning the racks and displays for the latest fashion trends. After hours of browsing and trying on clothes, I can feel my energy draining. Grabbing Claire's arm, I lean into whisper. "Are we at the museum part of your list yet?"

"Almost," she whispers back, shooting me a look of sympathy.

"Ugh," I groan, loud enough that Iris and Amanda send worried glances my way from where they are walking ahead of us. "My feet ache."

Amanda laughs. "But just think of the amazing new clothes you have, Avalina! We've only got a couple of more spots until lunch, anyway."

We are at a swanky boutique, with Iris and Claire oohing over all the shiny bits and baubles, while Amanda desperately tries to rope me into a conversation that I don't want to be a part of.

"Look at this floral top, Avie!" Amanda holds up a cream, sleeveless tank with pale blue and pink flowers swirling all over it. "You should totally get it!"

"Iris already talked me into that green dress. And I don't have a job right now, remember? I don't need any more clothes."

"But it has flowers on it!" Amanda pouts. "And you love flowers! You just need a boyfriend who will buy you clothes and then you won't need to worry about having a job."

"Is that your plan with Rick?" Claire asks as she walks over to see the top Amanda is holding.

"Of course," Amanda replies, "like that isn't your plan with Bobby."

"I like my job at the art gallery. I'd keep it even if Bobby gave me all his money."

Amanda rolls her eyes. "Not me. I can't wait to just buy clothes for myself instead of other rich people."

I can't shake the feeling that my friends were trying to mold me back into who I used to be. That they hoped I would simply slip back into my old self with a few spa treatments and shopping sprees. But with each step today, I feel the weight of who I used to be growing heavier, until it threatens to crush the person I'm still discovering.

"Avie, over here, look at this." Amanda pulls me to her. "What do you think of this necklace? I think it would look gorgeous with that green velvet dress you picked up." She holds the necklace up to my neck, squinting as if she could imagine the green dress in question on me and how it would look with the gems.

I have to admit, she is right. The necklace is a swirl of vines and flowers in rose gold and silver, adorned with tiny peridot and pink topaz gemstones cascaded to look like flowers on a vine. It matches perfectly with the green velvet dress with its sweetheart neckline and capped sleeves, gold thread woven over the skirt to look like falling leaves.

"It's beautiful, Amanda." My hand automatically moves to my necklace, the one I've been wearing since the accident.

I toy with it while debating how to respond. Amanda is obviously trying to connect with me, and she has no idea that the only necklace I have an interest in wearing is the one I'm currently toying with.

I also have no idea where I am going to wear that green velvet dress, as gorgeous as it is. Parties, galas, and balls no longer interest me. I just want to curl up with some hot tea and a good book.

I freeze as I realize I have gone on my mental tangent for too long and all the girls are staring at me, waiting for me to say something else.

"You know, I think you're right. It would look fantastic with that green dress." I smile at Amanda, hoping my anxiety at my delay isn't too noticeable. She is trying to connect with me in the only way I think she knows how, and I should meet her halfway. "But where would I wear it?"

Amanda smiles brightly, clearly in her element. "Oh, the Preston Gala at the end of the month! I'm sure we have enough time to find you a date between now and then, too!"

I blink, caught off guard. Going from talking about dresses to dates felt like diving into a near frozen lake, a shock to the system. I understand that this was the norm for Amanda, but all my bones rattle in a warning I do my best to ignore.

Once again, it feels like I'm donning a mask and playing pretend, unable to shake off this costume I have worn for so long.

Growing up in Kingsdale, wealth was power and everyone wanted to offer theirs up on a glittering display. There were always elaborate events to attend and outlandish donations to be made. Even birthday parties were monumental events. My parents, as lovely as they are, can't fathom the idea of a simple gathering with cake and presents. I remember my 10th birthday party was a tea party. At a 5-star hotel with an actual horse drawn carriage. It carried us around the hotel to the elaborate gardens where petite fours and ice sculptures awaited us. My 18th birthday is the last birthday I remember. It was a luxury wellness retreat in wine country, with private yoga and a hot-air balloon ride.

This getaway is just like those parties, elaborate and not at all in accord to who I feel I am now. The weight of familiarity hangs heavy on my shoulders, dragging me through endless rows of stores and through meaningless conversations. The laughter and energy of my friends echo around me, but I can't shake the feeling of being a puzzle piece that no longer fits in this picture-perfect world.

We decide to wrap up our day with some relaxation in a luxurious cafe, the scent of coffee and herbal teas wafting through the air. The laughter of my friends fills the air, but it sounds foreign to me, like a language I no longer understand. With all the chatter around me about parties and gossip, the latest fashion trends, and meaningless drama. I feel like an outsider, unable to take part in their conversations or share their excitement.

"Hey, Avalina," Amanda leans over the table, her eyes shining with anticipation. "Remember that night we snuck into the club and danced on the tables? That was wild, right?"

I rack my brain for any fragment of memory, but all I can muster is a vague recollection of flashing lights and deafening music. "I'm sorry, I don't remember," I admit softly, feeling a pang of disappointment in my chest.

"Ah, don't worry about it," she replies with a dismissive wave of her hand. "You'll be back to your old self in no time."

"Well, that's what this trip is all about!" Iris chimes in. "Making new memories with your friends. Right, Avie?"

"Right." I nod. But I don't want to be my old self - not anymore. I know that with an echo in my bones. Surrounded by these familiar faces, I suddenly long for the serenity of the woods, the scent of damp earth and the soothing rustle of leaves. My heart aches with the desire to follow my own path, even if it means leaving behind everything I once knew.

Once we return home, the promised matchmaking from Amanda begins in earnest. A ding interrupts the baking show that Iris and I are watching, and I look at my phone, face falling as I read the text from Amanda.

"Wait, she was serious?" I exclaim as I scroll through the questionnaire about what I look for in a man, including the size of his 401k.

"Who was serious?" Iris asks as she leans over my shoulder to peer at my screen.

"Amanda!" I practically shout as I shove the phone in her direction. "Look at this! She wants to set me up on a date for the Preston Gala. Ugh, that's the last thing I need right now."

Iris grabs the phone from me and swipes through the messages. "I don't see what's so bad about it. Amanda's just trying to help you get back to normal, to feel comfortable in your life again."

"Iris, there is a questionnaire! About who I want to date! Who does that?"

"Literally every dating app."

I groan. "It just feels so, ugh, I don't know... I just don't feel like dating."

"The rest of us have dates for the gala. Amanda just doesn't want you to feel left out."

"You think this is a good idea?" I stare at my sister.

"It couldn't hurt. I don't know why you're being so weird about it."

I frown, uncertainty weighing me down. Maybe my sister is right and I am just overreacting. I continue watching the show with Iris until she heads out to meet her boyfriend for lunch.

All the interference from my friends has my brain spiraling, and my mind feels like a dog with a bone it just won't let go of. I figure getting into a new environment will help, so I grab my things and head to one of my favorite places, the library.

Walking downtown, I can't help but admire the way the oak and maple trees are shifting colors, their green foliage giving way to autumn hues. They accent the picturesque stone streets of Kingsdale and brick buildings, some with little iron gated gardens out front. The library is on the same side of town as my apartment, surrounded by ancient trees and a mix of old and new architecture. On the outskirts of this part of the city there are some farms, and you can find a farmers market each weekend at Fox Lane Park across from the library. Head east and you enter the newer section of Kingsdale, with high-rise buildings, a hospital, and the River Arts District, where there are artists' workshops, restaurants, and museums.

Entering the library, I head straight for my favorite table and sit down, ignoring the buzz in my pocket. It's probably Amanda texting me again, asking me what kind of date I'm interested in for the gala. That is a conversation I'm not ready to have. Instead, I pull out my laptop and scroll through job listings.

My parents have graciously been covering my expenses since the accident, but I know I need to stand on my own two feet again. The art gallery has offered my old position back, but with no recollection of art history from before the accident, it feels like playing a role instead of being myself. Before and after the accident, that's how I divide my life.

"Is everything alright, Avalina?" A gentle voice asks from behind me. I turn to see Sarah, the head librarian. "You seem... troubled." Sarah is taller than me, and she leans down to place her russet skinned hand on my shoulder, her brown eyes filled with concern.

Nodding to buy time, I debate on how to answer. I don't want to trouble Sarah with my restless thoughts. "I'm just trying to find where I fit in," I confess, my voice tight from the weight of feeling like I was disappointing everyone around me. "How can I get my life back on track and find a job if I can't remember the past five years?"

"Hmm... that sounds rough," she says softly, placing a comforting hand on my shoulder. "Not everyone is expecting you to return to your old life, you know. You could try something new."

"Like what?"

"Why not work here? Mavis is about to go on parental leave, and I could use someone to step in for her while she's gone. You know how the library works and you're smart, you'll catch on quickly. Plus, you're here all the time, anyway." She says this last part with a smile.

"Oh, really? I mean, I'm sure there are others more qualified than me who need this position..."

Sarah interrupts my thoughts. "Nonsense. I wouldn't offer if I didn't think you were up to it. We could start with a two-week trial and see how things go."

"Wow. Okay, I mean, yes. Yes, I'd love that." I say, my heart swelling with gratitude.

"Then it's settled. Can you be here tomorrow at 8am? I'll give you a quick rundown on how things work before we open."

"Yes, I can do that."

"Sounds great. I'll see you then," she replies with a warm smile, squeezing my shoulder gently before returning to her duties.

Standing among the towering shelves of books, I feel the fluttering of hope for the first time in a while. The library was morphing before my eyes, shifting from a place of refuge to one of wonder, where I could grow and explore, unburdened by expectations and judgments.

Sarah is giving me a truly precious gift. Space to discover who I am now, away from the prying eyes of my parents and friends who expect the old me to emerge from the cocoon of the wreckage. But I'm not so sure anymore who I am transforming into or what color my wings will shine when I finally break free.

Chapter 5

Avalina

After a few days at the library, I'm beginning to feel *alive* again. It feels like my life is back on track. Maybe this is what I have been missing from before, a routine that grounds me and helps me feel like I am doing something with my days other than trying to recover the person I was before.

Logging out of my station at the circulation desk, I look up to see Mavis walking over, pushing a cart stacked high with books.

"Oh Avalina, I'm so glad that you accepted Sarah's job offer! I kept telling her she needed to find help while I was on maternity leave and stop trying to shoulder the weight of the world herself." Mavis grins from ear to ear, her light brown skin radiant against the fuzzy pink sweater covering her baby bump.

I chuckle. "You know how Sarah is." Sarah has been the head librarian here since I was in middle school, and she is the one who helped me discover my love of reading. I would walk here almost every day after school and curl up in one of the overstuffed chairs with a book.

"That I do." Mavis nods, her hand coming to rest on the swell of her belly. She notices me packing up my things. "You headed out?"

"Yes, Amanda set me up on a date."

Mavis's eyes widen. "You don't sound so excited."

"I'm not," I admit, feeling a wave of frustration wash over me. "It's just... hard for me to connect with people after my accident, explaining to them that there are years I don't remember."

Mavis nods understandingly. "I bet it can be tough, especially when you feel you're carrying the burden of your past with you." She pauses for a moment before continuing, "But maybe it's worth giving this guy a chance? You never know what might happen."

Her words strike a chord within me. Maybe I had been too quick to judge Amanda for her idea of dipping my toe back into the dating pool.

"You're right," I said decisively, surprising myself. "You never know what could happen."

Mavis smiles encouragingly. "Good for you. And if it doesn't work out, at least you can say that you gave it a shot."

I wrap my arms around Mavis. "Thank you. Even though I know that, sometimes it doesn't feel that way."

Mavis returns my hug before going back to her cart. "I'm going to go get these shelved. See you tomorrow!" she waves.

I wave back before weaving my way through the cavernous library, ready to go meet my date.

An hour later I'm at the best steakhouse in the city with Mickey James, sipping my sweet tea, and again wondering what on earth Amanda was thinking when she set up this date.

"So, Mickey, what do you like to do in your free time?"

"Oh, you know, go to the gym, check on my stocks. The yacht at my summer house is great. Nothing beats getting out on the water."

"I'm partial to the forest myself, but I bet the water is lovely."

"Are you into any sports? The Giants are looking good so far this year. They finally have a decent defense."

"So I've heard." I just keep nodding as Mickey talks, hoping something he says will interest me.

"Do you have investments? I was telling my friend, you have to watch out for the quad witching in the next month," Mickey continues on, unheeding of my blank look at his talk of the financial markets. "That, plus the ER, which should be coming out soon. It's bound to shake some of those paper hands out of their positions."

I blink, stunned into silence at Mickey's rambling.

"Anyway, are you going to the Preston Gala?" Mickey asks as he looks me up and down, like he's trying to figure out what size dress I wear.

I mentally cringe. "Yes, Amanda insists I go. And you know how Amanda is when she gets an idea in her head."

"I do. But I'm glad she suggested this."

I don't say anything, mentally struggling to keep up with the conversation, so Mickey continues. "I'd love to go to the gala with you. I know you'll look beautiful in a dress."

As I glance at my dark wash jeans, black ballet flats, and green cashmere sweater, my frustrations with Mickey are on the verge of boiling over.

Thankfully, I'm saved from throwing something at Mickey when the server comes over and asks if we want dessert.

"No, thank you, just the check please, split." I quickly interrupt Mickey before he can utter a single word, itching with the need to get out of here and demand Amanda come to her senses.

Mickey, oblivious to what had just happened, or perhaps thinking he could still charm me, reaches over the table to grab my hand that was resting near my tea. "Avalina, I'd like to see you again. How about we go up to my family's summer home this weekend?"

It takes all I have in me not to yank my hand away and snarl. *Who did this guy think he was?*

I plaster what I hope is a smile on my face. To be honest, it feels like a grimace.

"Mickey, I had a lovely time with you, but really, I'm just here because of Amanda. I'm really not looking for a relationship right now."

Mickey's face falls. "Oh, well..."

The server interrupts him, returning with our checks. I hand over some bills, wanting to get out of here as fast as possible, practically tripping over my feet as I stand and walk away.

All of this rushing has me not paying attention to my surroundings as I'm leaving the restaurant and I head straight into what feels like a brick wall. Turns out it is just a well-muscled chest.

"I'm so sorry," I sputter, scrambling to right myself and my purse. "I wasn't paying attention and..."

"Relax, Avalina, it's fine."

Everything in me freezes at the sound of that voice. It rings through me like a bell, but I'm not sure if it was chiming my celebration or my doom.

I look up, words forgotten. "Kieran."

Eyes the color of whiskey look down at me from above high cheekbones and a firm jaw. Dressed in black slacks and a dress shirt, Kieran exudes power and danger. But there's also a vulnerability as his gaze meets mine, a flicker of longing that tugs at my heart.

"Here." Kieran offers his arm. "I'll walk you to your car."

My brows furrow. "How do you know that's where I'm going?" I say, looking sideways at him as he steps beside me, obviously waiting for me to take his outstretched arm.

Kieran shrugs, placing his hands in his pocket instead. "Just a guess. You left the restaurant so quickly, I figured you wanted to get out of here in a hurry."

"Oh." Nervously, I fish my keys out of my purse as we round the corner to where my car is parked, unsure of what is happening and why Kieran is here.

Kieran glances away and his jaw flexes, like he is fighting himself not to say the words that want to tumble from his lips. After a moment, he looks back, saying, "I know you don't remember me. But we were friends. Before."

"I'm sorry I don't remember," was all I could manage in reply.

Kieran's eyes flash with a bright anger that seeps through his words. "Don't be sorry, Avalina. Never be sorry for that."

I swallow, unsure of what to say. Kieran seems to be the only one who doesn't make me feel ashamed or guilty that I can't remember. He seems to be willing to just let it be and move on, with no expectations.

He cocks his head and looks at me, his gaze seeing through the mask no one else dares to think is even there.

"Why were you at the restaurant, anyway?"

"My friend Amanda set me up on the date. She's trying to find me a date for the Preston Gala."

An eyebrow arches. "Is that what you want? A date to the gala?"

I shrug. "I'm fine going on my own."

"Then tell Amanda that. Use those words that you love to read."

Something slithers down my spine at his command, but I refuse to examine it. "Well," I say brightly, "thank you for walking me to my car. You didn't have to do that."

An emotion crosses his features, there and gone before I can name it. "Someone has to keep an eye out for you."

Shrugging off his overprotective comment, I unlock my car and ease behind the wheel. Backing out of the parking space, I feel the burning intensity of Kieran's eyes on me the entire time.

Chapter 6

Avalina

I want to unravel the mystery of Kieran and understand why he seems to keep showing up in my life. Why looking at him feels like my missing memories and fragmented friendships don't matter. I've asked my friends, even my boss Sarah, what they know of Kieran Calder. Their reactions range from surprise to annoyance that I'm asking about him.

My sister bristles when I mention his name. "The Calder's... they're dangerous. They pretty much control Kingsdale. The rumors are that they are a mob family. Why are you asking about Kieran, anyway?" Iris peers at me.

I realize I may be stumbling upon something bigger than I bargained for.

"Why do you think they're dangerous?" I ask Iris, trying to keep my voice steady.

"I've heard things," she says, her eyes darting around as if she's afraid someone might be listening. "Whispers about shady deals and illegal activities. And people who try to cross them...well, let's just say it doesn't end well and they disappear."

My mind races with possibilities. Could Kieran be involved in these activities? Or is he just an innocent member of the notorious Calder family?

As if reading my thoughts, Iris adds, "I've seen him around town with his brother. They always seem to be up to something." Her eyes narrow and I get the sense that she is going to lecture me like I'm not the older sister. "You should stay away from him, Avalina. Nothing good comes from the Calders."

The threat from Iris just makes me want to investigate more.

Later that day, as I'm working at the library, I ask my co-workers what they think of Kieran.

"Kieran Calder?" Mavis frowns. "He mostly keeps to himself, him and his family. No one really knows much about them."

Even my boss, Sarah, tries to warn me away. "It's best to stay away from the Calders. They're trouble, and I don't want you to get caught up in their mess."

Her words only fuel my curiosity even more. Who are the Calders, and why are they so feared?

I can't resist the urge to do some research on the Calders on the library computer. After hours of digging through old newspaper articles and online forums, I come across an interesting piece of information–Kieran's father, Anthony Calder, was once arrested for racketeering but was released due to lack of evidence.

Could this be why everyone is so wary of the Calders? Is Kieran following in his father's footsteps?

I try to brush off their warnings and vague comments, but it only makes me more curious. I had seen Kieran and his brother Liam in the restaurant the other night, and something about him had captivated me. It wasn't just his rugged good looks or his magnetic dark eyes. There is something else that draws me to him.

Since then, my dreams have been filled with Kieran - his powerful arms around me, full lips claiming mine. It both scares and thrills me all at once. And during the day, I swear I can feel his eyes on me as I go about my daily routine.

But despite my curiosity and attraction towards Kieran, my friends refuse to tell me anything more about him. So I decide to take matters into my own hands and find out about him myself.

I take the long way into town, still not able to drive the same route that I had my accident on. It takes longer to get anywhere this way, but I have fewer nightmares. Heading into town, my eyes scan the streets and shops for anyone who might have insight into the elusive Kieran Calder.

As I pass the bar that I ran into Kieran a couple of weeks ago, an idea comes to me. Bartenders are known to be fonts of gossip and rumor. Surely someone there has stories to share if plied with a drink or two.

I pull into the parking lot and make my way inside the dimly lit bar, the fragrance of stale beer permeating the air. I'm not the only one here, and other patrons dot the bar counter, with a few more having lunch at the tables.

"What can I get you, lass?" the bartender asks in his gruff voice.

"Oh, just an iced tea for now, thanks," I say as I slide onto a bar stool.

He raises an eyebrow but pours my drink without comment. As I take a sip, I gather my nerve.

"I was wondering if you could help me with something," I begin casually. "I'm trying to find out some information about Kieran Calder."

The bartender's eyes widen briefly before his expression turns guarded. "Can't say I know much about him or his family. They keep to themselves mostly."

I study his face, certain he knows more than he's admitting. I lean in conspiratorially, pulling a $20 dollar bill from my jeans pocket and sliding it across the counter.

"Please, I'd be very grateful for anything you could tell me. I'm just so fascinated by him," I say, infusing my voice with as much innocent allure as I can muster.

The bartender hesitates, then relents. "Not much to tell, really. The Calders have lived here for ages, but don't mingle with the townsfolk."

He polishes a glass, then adds quietly, "Best steer clear of Kieran, though. He has a dangerous air about him."

Just then, a burly patron at the end of the bar overhears our conversation and interjects gruffly, "You're asking about Kieran Calder? Watch yourself around that one; he's not someone you want to cross." His words hang ominously in the air as he takes another swig of his drink.

My heart races as the patron's words sink in. What does everyone mean by "watch yourself" around Kieran? I can't help but feel drawn to him, but now I'm starting to question if that's a good thing.

Before I can ask any further questions, the patron finishes his drink and leaves without another word. The bartender looks at me with a mix of pity and caution, as if he knows something he's not telling me.

"Is there something you're not telling me about Kieran?" I press, hoping against hope that he'll crack under my persistent questioning.

But the bartender just shakes his head. "I've said all I know. Now why don't you leave this alone before you get yourself into trouble."

I sigh in frustration and finish my iced tea. It seems like no one wants to tell me anything about Kieran, and those who do only warn me to stay away from him. But the more people try to scare me off, the more determined I become to uncover his secrets.

Leaving the pub, I decide to take a walk around town in hopes of stumbling upon someone else who might have information about Kieran Calder. But as I stroll through the quaint streets and charming shops, it seems like everyone is purposely avoiding talking about him.

Feeling defeated, I make my way back home as dusk settles over the horizon.

Chapter 7

Avalina

I'm getting ready to go for a morning walk in the woods when I knock sounds at my door. I open it to find Amanda standing there, dressed in the latest Saturday fashion trend of tan ankle boots with distressed jeans and a pale pink slouchy sweater. She looks like effortless grace, but I know that casual look costs hundreds.

She smiles brightly as she holds up a tray of to-go coffees and a paper bag. "I thought since you've been too busy to text me back that I'd come to you. And I brought treats."

"Text you back?" I ask, trying to catch up with what Amanda is saying as I move back to let her into my apartment. Amanda sets the treats on my coffee table, unwrapping the bag and handing me a coffee before nestling into the couch, turning so she can look at me while she talks.

"About Mickey! How did the date go? I want to know all the details. Has he asked you to the Preston Gala yet? Because if he hasn't, I've got some other date ideas."

I accept the coffee, cradling the warmth in my hands, and sink into the other side of the couch, pulling my knees up to my chest. "It was... underwhelming," I begin, hesitating. "Mickey seemed more interested in his stock portfolio, his parents' summer house in the Hamptons, and how I fit into a dress than he was in anything I had to say."

"I'm sure he was just nervous," Amanda suggests, pushing a chocolate croissant towards me. "Maybe he just rambles when he's nervous and was talking about things he knows well."

"Perhaps," I begin before Amanda cuts me off.

"You need to give him another chance. I know you two could hit it off. Give him another shot at the Preston Gala."

I nibble on the pastry, its sweetness failing to mask the dull ache of disinterest. The thought of enduring another night with Mickey, with his smug smile and roving eyes that undressed me rather than seek out the soul beneath, is nearly unbearable. Yet Amanda's hopeful gaze pins me down, a gentle yet insistent pressure.

"I don't know, Amanda," I sigh. "I don't think Mickey and I are the right fit for each other. He's interested in things I'm not."

"It's not like you need to marry him, Avalina! Just go with him to the Preston Gala. Everyone else has a date, and I don't want you to feel left out."

"Okay," I begrudgingly reply, knowing that what I crave isn't the shallow sparkle of gala gowns and forced laughter. It's the earthy embrace of the forest, the soft touch of moss under my fingertips, and the mysterious pull an enigma named Kieran Calder, who haunts my dreams with stormy eyes and a passion that whispers of forbidden longing.

Amanda beams as if I've just handed her the keys to the castle, oblivious to my own inner turmoil. "I was hoping you would say that!" she exclaims as she pulls a stack of magazines from her giant shoulder bag.

"What are those?" I ask, setting down my coffee and croissant, trepidation crawling its way up my spine.

"I thought we could look through these for ideas for your hair and makeup! You already have the dress, so it's just a matter of finalizing your look."

My mind flashes back to the green velvet dress that my sister convinced me to pick up when we had on our girls weekend away. It is a gorgeous dress, and I have to admit that I am looking forward to wearing it. Even though it is an evening gown, and represents a part of my life I feel no longer fits me, the gold thread woven through the hem and draping skirt looks like falling leaves, a nod to my love of nature and the safety I feel in the forest.

Even Amanda had caught onto the reasons why I gravitated towards the dress, encouraging me to purchase a necklace during our trip that looked like little pink and green flowers on a vine.

Watching Amanda sort through her magazines, looking for just the right one, I can feel myself being torn in opposite directions. I want to feel close to Amanda, the way I must have felt before the accident snatched away my memories of our friendship. I understand that Amanda feels at home in the world of fashion, and this is her way of connecting to me.

But a part of me, one I don't completely understand or recognize, rebels at this part I'm playing. This inner version of me feels like a wild thing, savage and untamed in her ferocity, refusing to be put in a box that limits her freedom.

I know that part of me is there, but I also recognize that I'm just not ready to admit it, not really. As much as the dresses and gala chaff, as much as they feel constraining and restricting, there is a comfort in sticking to what I know.

Reaching for my coffee, I take a sip to buy myself some time, the idea of walking myself willinging into a cage as bitter as the coffee.

"Do you have some ideas? I don't know what's in style anymore..." I trail off, the unspoken reference to my missing memories an opening that Amanda latches onto.

"Oh, yes!" she exclaims, flipping through the magazine to look for an image she had marked with a sticky note. Turning the glossy page towards me, she points with a manicured nail. "I was thinking this hairstyle would look amazing with your dress and face, it will really bring out your eyes."

I nod and murmur my assent, grateful that I'm connecting with Amanda, but wondering why I still feel like I'm lost at sea.

Chapter 8

Kieran

Finn receives word that Rocco still isn't behaving after our little chat, so we make our way down to Rocco's Cabaret on a quiet Wednesday afternoon. The fallen leaves crunch under my shoes as we walk towards the double doors stained a dark brown. The building itself is a bit garish, looking more like the ancient pantheon with its white plaster columns supporting the triangular roof.

Finn leads the way inside. I scare people because of the whispers that run rampant of my torture methods, but Finn is scary just because he is like myth made flesh, a huge wall of muscle and bone.

Glancing around, I don't see Rocco anywhere, but Michelle, one of the girls that works at the strip club, is cleaning tables. Finn turns on his charm and waltzes over.

"Hey Michelle, is Rocco around?" he asks, resting his arms on the table she was cleaning.

Michelle straightens, glancing at me before turning to Finn. "He's not here. Why are you looking for him?"

"We are concerned that some of management's decisions are negatively affecting the staff's morale."

A harsh laugh escapes Michelle, but I recognize the flash of fear that crosses her face as she tries to turn her laugh into a cough.

So does Finn. He tilts his head. "Maybe you can help us. Tell us what you know."

Her head is shaking before she even begins backing away. "I'm not getting in the middle of this. I've worked too hard and long to become a manager here so I don't have to be on the floor every night. I'm not risking it for some asshole." Michele says, glancing around.

I hold up my hands, stepping around Finn. "I promise we can keep you safe. We can keep everyone safe, but only if we know what's going on."

"You'll have to kill him to keep us safe."

"I know."

Michelle sighs, sitting down in one of the chairs.

Sitting across from Rocco, I pick up a blade, twirling it between my fingers.

Despite my desire to put my family on a better path, there is darkness within me. And perhaps that is why I so strongly believe in a better way. That way I can pretend that in my heart I'm not the biggest monster of them all.

The killing, the darkness, the blood. In it, I find the silence I crave. In it, the beast within is soothed. The only other thing that quiets the inner desire is Avalina. But she is no longer mine.

So, death was my answer to the demons that swirled under my skin. My beast needed to be let out of his cage.

I inhale deeply, savoring the feel of letting the reins of control go, feeling the tightness in my skin give way to a pleasurable hum in my blood.

Bending my neck to one side and then the other, I smile, feeling like I could breathe for the first time in months. I wanted nothing more than to feel like this always.

Pointing my knife to the stack of passports Finn and I found in Rocco's office, I sigh. "Let's try this again, Rocco. Why the passports?"

"Who the fuck told you about the passports?"

"What matters is what you tell me about them. I already gave you a second chance. Do you think you're going to get a third?"

"Besides," Finn looks up from where he's sitting with Rocco's laptop, combing through the hard drive, "I'm sure you've heard the rumors about Kieran. Do you really want him to do that shit to you?

Tell us what we want to know and I'll make sure you get a quick death."

"Motherfuckers, I'm going to kill you!" Rocco screams, his face turning as red as the blood I was hoping would be dripping on the floor soon.

I turn to Finn, shrugging. "I guess he wants torture, then."

"No!" Rocco yells. "God, no. I'll tell you. I'll tell you."

Turning back to Rocco, I gesture with my blade still dancing between my fingers. "Go on."

"The passports, they're insurance, okay? So the girls won't talk."

"And what would they talk about? Tea parties and nail salons?"

"Fuck. They're trafficked okay? Sean runs a circuit where girls come in on ships or he kidnaps them and he places them in his businesses." Finn and I exchange a glance as Rocco keeps spilling the beans. "He keeps their passports as collateral. They're trapped. We pay them peanuts, so they have no way out."

"And that shipment coming in next week? It's not guns?" Finn asks.

"It's girls." Rocco sighs, hanging his head. But I know it's not in shame, but rather he thinks because he told us what we wanted that he'll be let off the hook. He's relieved.

Rage pummels through me, hot and heavy, and I'm moving to bend down towards Rocco before I can process the thought, my blade stabbing into his crotch.

Rocco bellows, surprise flashing across his features while my cold stare drinks in his agony as my knife saws deeper. Behind me, I hear Finn mutter, "So much for a quick death."

Chapter 9

KIERAN

I can't tear my thoughts away from Avalina. Seeing her around town, seeing her on dates. I grit my teeth. I know I need to let her go, but the tether tying me to her is knotted tighter than ever.

Throughout our time together, one thing was obvious: Avalina wanted out of this town and out of the socialite life she felt cornered into by her parents and friends. She felt trapped and wanted nothing more than to fly away.

I'm not about to stop her now, no matter how much I want her to be mine. A pretty cage is still a cage, after all.

The amber liquid burns as it slides down my throat. I savor the slow, spreading heat, hoping it will thaw the numbness that has taken hold since the accident.

Avalina.

Her name echoes through my mind, piercing my heart like a shard of glass. I shouldn't think of her, not like this.

But god help me, I want her. Desire her with an intensity that leaves me shaking. I want to run my fingers through her silken hair, to caress every inch of her porcelain skin, to kiss those petal-soft lips until neither of us can breathe...

I slam my glass down, the crystal ringing out sharply in the silence. This is madness. She is no longer mine. I have a duty to keep her safe, nothing more.

So why does the thought of her returning to her old life make my chest tighten painfully? Why does the memory of her smile, so open and warm, make me crave things best left in the dark?

I glance down at the paperwork on my desk, trying to focus on the task at hand instead of getting lost in my anger and fantasies. I hate this room. It was my father's and being in it brings back memories I would rather forget.

The first thing I did when I took over for the family was to get rid of everything in this room and fill it with things that felt more like me.

But the aged wood and leather chairs don't replace the memories I would rather forget. The walls still remember.

A knock on my door has me glancing up in time to see Cassandra stroll in.

Another difference between me and my father. Cassandra is my second, something my father would have never allowed. To him, a woman's place was the house and home. Being a wife and mother. That's all they could be. Such fucking nonsense.

Cassandra is something I can't be - stealthy, unassuming, and even more importantly, subtle. People underestimate her, and she has a charm she can turn on that gets her out of all kinds of tough spots. In this way, we work well as a team.

People also assume that there is tension between me and Liam since he isn't my second. Liam doesn't want this life any more than I do, so we use that preconceived notion to our advantage when we can.

Cassandra drops into the leather chair across from my desk, sliding one knee across the other. Her blonde hair is braided away from her face today, showcasing her pale skin with a constellation of freckles across her cheeks.

"Any new updates?" I ask as I push the pile of paperwork to the side of my desk. It isn't getting done, anyway.

"Just that Sean's men were spotted down by the docks, unloading cargo like we suspected. I think we should continue to work with Finn to uncover what they're up to. They're trying to keep it under wraps, so you know it's nothing good."

"Agreed." Cassie, Liam, and I have been working with Finn to undermine his father's illegal dealings. We have to be smart to not tip off Sean O'Neil that it is his own son ratting him out.

So far, we've been selective in what business we disrupt, keeping Sean on his toes, and guessing who or what is behind the chaos. It means we can't stop everything, and sometimes that thought burns through me, leaving the bitter taste of ash on my tongue.

I sit back in my chair, watching Cassie slip a small knife from her propped up boot and start picking dirt from under her nails.

"The Hartwell accident. I want you to look into it again."

Umber eyes blink at me in surprise, then suspicion, her hands frozen midair. "Avalina's accident? Why? We know there was foul play, the brake lines were cut, but there weren't any leads."

"I know, but it's been a few months since it happened. Maybe someone talked. Bragged. She was targeted and I want to know why."

She shrugs, not one to argue unless she feels she has a winning hand. "Okay. Anything else I should know?"

I get up and pour another drink, trying to buy myself some time. I know Cassandra has her suspicions, but there isn't anything to tell now. Not really. Avalina and I don't have a relationship anymore. She doesn't even remember me. I'm the one haunted by ghosts of memories that no longer exist.

"Nope." I reply, turning towards her while bringing the whiskey to my lips.

Cassandra says nothing, just rises out of her chair and begins to make her way out of the room.

"Oh, I almost forgot," she says as she pauses with a hand on the doorknob and turns back to me. "Avalina's going to the Preston Gala. With Mickey James. Just thought you'd want to know."

Cassandra throws a smile my way before practically skipping out the door, heedless of the bomb she just tossed my way and the damage it would bring.

I can't stop the hiss that escapes my clenched jaw. Who am I kidding? I never can hide anything from Cassie. She knows my obsession with Avalina hasn't gone away. And Mickey James? As irrational as it is, I don't want to let him touch what is mine. I can feel my monster rear its head, the craving to rip Mickey into pieces that no one will ever find rushing through me.

I can feel my blood boil, and I breathe deeply through my nose to regain my composure. Closing my eyes, I feel a shudder run through my body. I know what I have to do.

The dim lights of the warehouse make it hard to see unless you are standing right next to their small circle of illumination, but luckily, I know exactly where everything is. Like I told Liam, if you put things back in the same place each time, it makes life much easier.

Sean is becoming a problem, and one I intend to solve. But dealing with the leader of the O'Neil family is a long game, and I have to keep my head on my shoulders to win.

My mind keeps drifting to the gala and Avalina. And Mickey. Part of me wants to visit Mickey and have a talk, but that would get me nowhere. Avalina is smart, and she'd figure out it was me, eventually.

I don't mind the questions, and I can deal with suspicion. I cover my tracks well, after all.

What I want to avoid is Avalina looking at me like I am a monster. She never did before, and I don't want to give her any reason to do so now.

But Mickey, he is bad news. Everyone knows he is an asshole that has an ego the size of the eastern seaboard. Despite the compulsion to swoop in and protect Avalina, I know she can take care of herself. I have to trust that and not go after Mickey myself. For now, I have to sate my beast another way.

Wrapping a length of corded rope around my arm, I arrange it into a neat coil, tucking one end into the other so it will stay in place.

Maybe if I tie my heart up in enough knots, I will stop feeling like I am still bound to Avalina.

I grin, eager to shift my mind from the past, to numb my soul from the pain that echoes within it daily. Here I can escape all of that.

I slap the cheek of the unconscious man before me, one of Sean's goons. He stirs, but I'm not in a pleasant mood, so I slap the other cheek just to get the message across. I hope I didn't spike his drink too much. It was never fun when I didn't get to play.

"What?" Paul moans, blinking. I lean into his space and grip his chin, impatient to get started.

He jerks, trying to move his body, startled as he realizes I tied him to the chair. "What the fuck? What is this?" he exclaims, his words becoming less slurred as adrenaline pumps through his veins. Hatred flares in his eyes as he looks at me. "Do you know who I am? I'm going to kill you for this!" He is yelling now, but there is no one around for miles, no one to hear him scream.

It wasn't hard to find him in his favorite bar, slinging back beers like they were water. It was easier still to spike his drink and follow him to his truck, just in time for him to pass out. His truck was now being torched, and his body would soon follow.

A calm washes over me as I step back to watch the man thrash. He is on my list, and tonight was just his lucky night.

Moving into the light, Paul finally sees my face and all his bravado comes to a screeching halt. "Calder. What do you want?" he sneers.

"A little bird told me you were up to no good, Paul." I tut as I walk around him, the knife in my hand catching the light as I move with my words.

"And you know how this works. Sean may not have any morals, but I do. And whatever the O'Neils think, it's the Calders that rule Kingsdale. So once I hear about trash in my town, I take it out." I whisper from behind him.

"I... I don't know what you're talking about, man." Paul stutters.

I don't bother to hide my hatred for him as I move back in front of him, my words staccato, like the quick hammering of nails. "Your daughter, Paul. You've been molesting your daughter."

"What? No, man, you've got it all wrong. Whatever she's told you, it's lies, I swear."

"Funny, that. Pictures don't lie."

"Please, please don't hurt me," Paul whimpers, a stain already darkening the front of his jeans. I smirk. I haven't even gotten started yet. Begging would get him nowhere. Not when I know what he has been doing to his daughter. I grip the knife tighter.

"Hmm... I wonder where we should start. " I slowly trace the tip of my blade down his cheek, leaving a thin trail of blood in my wake.

"Fuck, stop!" The whimpers morph into shouts as Paul tries to move his body away from me, which is going to be hard to do, considering the chair is bolted into the warehouse floor.

"You're going nowhere, Paul, so you might as well stop trying to escape." The threat in my voice was crystal clear.

"What do you want with me?"

"I would have thought that was clear by now."

"I'll give you whatever you want."

"What about your daughter? Can you give her back her childhood, her innocence?" I sneer. I may be a monster, but disgust rolls through me at the images I found on his computer, at the secret room he built for 'playtime' with his own child.

I am running out of patience with this little chat and want to get on with it.

Flicking my knife, I quickly swipe down, stabbing Paul right into his lying mouth.

The whimpers of the rotten man before me turn into a scream. I sigh, pulling my knife back. It is always like this.

The ones that do the most harm are the ones that can't take the heat. Such a fucking waste. Frowning, I lift my arm up before swiping across Paul's neck with my blade, sending him to a black oblivion.

This is my secret. This is why I can be the muscle of the Calder clan, why I prefer it rather than handing the job off to Liam or someone else. I kill those who need to be killed, those who abuse and lord their power over others for their personal gain. This allows me to keep my composure, allows me to stay level-headed when I can periodically feed the monster within.

The reputation I receive because of not shying away from dirty work is a plus. It makes folks think twice before crossing me, and I like to think it keeps my family safe.

Liam knows my preference to be the killer of our family, but he doesn't understand why, and I want to keep it that way. Even though Liam is an open book to me, I only pretend to be as much for him.

The only person I am an open book to is Avalina. Correction. The only person I *used* to be an open book to is Avalina, but those pages were ripped out the night of her accident.

Chapter 10

Avalina

Kieran consumes my thoughts like a spiderweb I can't shake off, but my focus is on the Preston Gala this evening and my date with Mickey. I've dreaded the event all week, yet another reminder of how out of place I've been feeling since I woke up confused and disoriented in the hospital. But I already had agreed and had the dress, so it felt cowardly of me to back out now.

Staring at my reflection in the mirror, I can't help but think maybe I should just be a coward and hide under my bedcovers for the rest of the night. A night of faces I can't remember talking to me about events I can't recall. I can't help but wonder what secrets are hidden in my gaze. What memories are locked in my mind.

The zip of my emerald gown weaves its silent song up the curve of my spine, Iris standing behind me, her deft fingers working the delicate fabric with care. The mirror reflects a stranger draped in elegance, her forest green eyes wide with a blend of anticipation and anxiety.

"Stop fidgeting, Avie," Iris chides gently, a smile tugging at her rosebud lips. The scent of her floral perfume mingles with the warm air of my apartment, settling like a promise on my skin. "You look breathtaking. Are you excited to see Mickey tonight?"

I smile and murmur my assent as Iris heads back to my closet to find shoes for the dress. While my thoughts about the gala should be about my date, they keep drifting and catching on the dark eyes of Kieran Calder.

Iris interrupts my thoughts when she pops out of my closet, holding up a pair of shiny gold heels.

"What about these?" she asks as I glance down at the green velvet dress draped across my body.

"Those will work," I reply absently, reaching out to grab the shoes. I bend down, putting my feet inside the strappy, glittering contraptions before securing them around my ankles.

Iris comes to stand behind me, assessing my reflection in the mirror as I shift to stand back up. I smile at Iris's gaze in the glass. Her short dark hair is slicked back, and a bright pink gauzy dress adorns her frame. It suits her personality, light and bubbly.

Glancing back at my reflection, I realize I'm dressed like the forest I so adore these days, the rich velvet a lovely shade of emerald.

Iris helped me with my hair, so the dark copper strands are curled delicately around my face. I reach up to take off the necklace I always wear, the rose gold gleaming in the early evening light.

I've often wondered what it means or why I have it, the pendant like a circle with two leaves on either side that weave their way inside the sphere. Looking down at the necklace in my hand, a wave of longing washes through me. For some reason, I don't want to part with the necklace, even though it would look out of place with the evening gown. I decide to wrap it around my wrist as a bracelet, a tether to the person I want to be, no matter how much my past seems to haunt me.

I clasp the gemstone necklace Amanda picked out around my neck. It feels too heavy and out of place there, like it's an anchor dragging me down. But I'm trying to fit in, trying to be a good friend to Amanda, and she picked out this necklace to go with my dress. And I know Amanda is trying too, and she picked the necklace with its flower and leaf design as a nod to my newfound love of the woods and all things nature.

I catch Iris' gaze in the mirror and give her a quick smile. I hope she can't see how tight it is at the edges. Finding my place in life again feels like attempting to wear a coat that is two sizes too small. No matter how much I tug and twist, it doesn't fit me.

I thought the job at the library, in a place surrounded by books I love, would be the answer, but there's still a strain, this chasm between me and my life that seems too large to cross.

The evening air is crisp as we arrive at the Preston Gala, the girls deciding we would ride together and meet our dates there. The grand facade of the building looming before us like a gothic masterpiece. The stone walls are adorned with intricate carvings of mythical creatures, their eyes seeming to follow our every move as we step out of the chauffeured car, the heavy wooden doors beckoning us inside.

I hang back, letting my friends walk ahead of me and admire the colorful picture they make. Claire in shimmery gold, Amanda in bold red, Jessica in a deep blue that she swears matches her finance's eyes, and Iris in her puffy pink dress.

I want to fit in. I want to belong with these women I watch walk ahead of me, but I feel further apart from them than ever, despite my attempts to find common ground and build comradery over the past weeks.

Shaking off the thoughts, I take large strides to catch up with my friends, my gold heels swishing the soft velvet around me.

Weaving my arm with Claire's, I beam up at my best friend, determined to shake off the feelings haunting me.

"You ready?" Claire glances at me, and I know she understands my trepidation as I nod and walk inside the building.

I can't stop the gasp that leaves my lips as I step inside the ballroom, which is like stepping inside another world.

They hold the Preston Gala here every year, but I don't have any memories of it.

The inside of the ballroom seems to glitter, with faux candles and gold accents. White flowers, including lilies and baby's breath, adorn the tables, and the twinkling lights almost make the atmosphere seem ethereal, like we're up in the clouds.

My mind flashes back to a book about angels, and I can't help but feel a little uncomfortable at how these people would adorn this space to reflect a heavenly, golden vibe, when the true good thing to do would have been to take this gala money and give it directly to a charity.

Doing my best to shove that line of thinking aside, knowing it would do nothing but further the divide I'm currently feeling, a turn to a server making the rounds and grab a glass of champagne off their tray. I barely restrain myself from swallowing the whole thing in one go and instead sip at the bubbly liquid, following Claire to a table.

As we all sit down, I catch glimpses of dazzling gowns and sparkling jewels. The space is alive with laughter and music, a symphony of voices and melodies filling the air.

My hand fiddles with the necklace curled around my wrist with little thought. Glancing down at it, I feel bolstered by a sense of strength that doesn't quite feel like my own. I take a deep breath and try to join in the conversation of my friends around me, despite the turmoil doing its best to drown everything out.

"What are we talking about?" I ask, peering at Claire, who is sitting next to me.

Claire smiles and answers, "The new Lorelei Crane exhibit coming to the art gallery."

"Oh," I say before Amanda interrupts me.

"You know, where you used to work. Don't you remember? You were the one that spearheaded the campaign to get Crane's work at the gallery."

My face falls at that. I don't remember. I *can't* remember. The hush that has fallen over the table tells me that the other girls know I don't remember as well. The color drains from Amanda's face, her mouth moving, but no sounds coming out.

I know she feels bad, but I just want to disappear, just melt into the floor. Thoughts race through my head about how I shouldn't have come here. I rather be in the forest, or the library, or at home with Conan. Anywhere but here where it feels like my skin is crawling with the need to escape and run away.

The moment feels like it stretches out forever, but I know it's only a couple of seconds of stilted silence before Claire and Iris are both talking at once, trying to steer the conversation to a safer topic.

I nod and smile, waving away Amanda's blunder, eager to forget that I can't remember, to pretend that this is where I belong and that I still fit in with my friends. It's a mask I'm becoming more and more at ease with wearing. The thought tickles the back of my mind like a scratch I can't itch, but I push it aside, shoving it into a mental box to deal with later.

As more and more people arrive, the soft music becomes louder, and more folks make their way to the dance floor.

As I watch, I realize I don't really know anyone here other than the girls sitting at the table with me. More thoughts about how I shouldn't be here attempt to escape the box in the back of my mind, so I add mental chains around the box to keep it closed.

"Would you care to dance?" The drawl interrupts my thoughts and I look up to see Mickey staring back at me, hand held out expectantly. I do my best to place a charming smile on my face.

Mickey's olive skin gleams under the candlelight, his hazel eyes framed by curly black hair. His tuxedo fits him like he was born to wear it, a stark contrast to the unease coiling within me. His smile doesn't quite reach his eyes as they settle on me, the appraisal in them unmistakable. Belatedly, I realize that Mickey's hand is still outstretched towards me. I scramble, widening my smile and placing my hand in his.

I feel like a robot, letting Mickey lead me to the dance floor. *What am I even doing here?* Before I can register what's happening, Mickey sweeps me in his arms and we're moving to the music, Mickey's hands settling possessively on my waist.

The effort to wipe the bored-I-rather-be-anywhere-but-here look from my face must not be working because Mickey looks confused, almost as if he is trying to fight a scowl. This evening isn't going at all how it was supposed to go and I can feel bright panic nipping at my heels, ready to devour me whole.

"You look uncomfortable, Avalina," he murmurs, his voice a low rumble above the music's embrace. "Is this too much for little ol' you?"

I falter, his condescension pricking at my already fragile composure. The warmth of his body against mine feels intrusive rather than comforting, and I can't shake the feeling of being a lamb trotted out for show among wolves.

"Maybe I'm just not used to all this," I admit, hoping for a sliver of understanding.

"Or maybe you just don't belong here," Mickey retorts, his smile now carrying a sharp edge.

His words sting, confirming my fears. Yet, despite the chill of his mockery, there's a fire within me that refuses to be extinguished—a fiery remnant of the woman I used to be, perhaps, or the one I am becoming. I lift my chin, determined not to let Mickey James, or anyone else, dictate where I belong.

Before I can say anything, a shadow looms over us and a voice I'd recognize anywhere interrupts.

"May I cut in?" Kieran's voice is steel wrapped in velvet, a dangerous combination that has my heart stumbling over its own rhythm.

Mickey's grip tightens, his smile now a sneer. "I don't recall her being yours to dance with, Calder."

"Maybe you've danced enough" Kieran replies, eyes locked onto mine. There's a silent plea there, a question he can't voice amidst the throng of high society.

"Keep dreaming," Mickey spits back, pulling me closer. His touch burns with possession, branding me as an object rather than a partner.

Kieran steps forward, and the space between the three of us charges with an electric current. "She's not your plaything, James."

"Since when do you care?" Mickey challenges, baring the fangs of his bruised ego.

"Since always," Kieran breathes, and his fist flies, connecting with Mickey's jaw in a crack that resonates louder than the crescendo of violins.

The crowd gasps, a collective intake of breath that sucks the warmth from the room. Mickey stumbles back, surprise etched into the lines of his face where a red mark blooms like a rose in winter. He touches his jaw, eyes wide with disbelief, then glares at Kieran with venomous defeat before disappearing into the sea of bodies.

Silence stretches, a taut string ready to snap, until Kieran extends his hand to me, palm open and inviting. "Dance with me, Avalina."

I place my hand in his, instinctively seeking the heat that promises sanctuary. The world fades into a backdrop as we find our rhythm, bodies moving in sync to a song that seems composed just for us. Kieran's hands are firm but gentle, guiding without dictating, a stark contrast to Mickey's earlier claims.

"You didn't have to do that," I whisper, caught in the orbit of his dark eyes.

"I did," he says simply, and I believe him.

Our dance is a conversation without words, every turn and dip a sentence spun from the language of desire. The spicy scent of his cologne wraps around me, a heady mix of power and mystery that I remember without knowing why.

"Thank you," I murmur, gratitude mingling with something deeper, something that feels like yearning.

"Anything for you," he replies, his voice a caress that ignites a fire deep within me, a fire I thought was long extinguished.

"What are you even doing here?" I gasp, my mind reeling with the events.

"A little bird told me you were going to be here, and I thought I'd join you."

"But, why?" I ask, perplexed.

Kieran doesn't answer. His eyes pierce mine with ruthless intensity. I want to look away but can't, feeling the strongest feeling of something just out of reach in the corner of my mind. A wave of déjà vu threatens to take me under.

"You know, I asked around about you."

"You did? And what did you find out?"

"Nothing. No one wants to talk about you." I can feel my eyes narrow and try to shove down my rising frustration at the lack of answers.

"Who are you?" I finally ask, my voice barely audible in the cavernous ballroom. His sensuous mouth curves into a knowing smile. I can't help but bite my own in response.

"I think you know, Avalina," he says, my name sounding intimate on his lips. His voice is a low caress.

My pulse quickens, and I feel my breath coming faster. I have the curious urge to reach out and touch him. I automatically reach up to toy with my necklace, but it's not there. It's on my wrist instead. I glance down at it, frowning. I can't help but notice how closely Kieran watches the movement.

"Do you like this necklace? I've noticed you look at it a lot."

"You always wear it. Why?"

I shrug. "It feels comforting, safe." I pause, unsure of my next words or why I want to voice them. But Kieran was the one that reminded me to use my words. "Was it from you?"

"Yes." he replies, voice strained with something I couldn't place.

"Why?"

"So you would remember me." His words were coated with a longing I recognized, but it terrifies me all the same.

Sensing my turmoil, he lifts a hand as if to touch my cheek but stops just shy of contact. Even that near caress sends heat flooding through me.

The song ends too soon, and Kieran steps aside, but not before bending to whisper in my ear. "Meet me in the woods tomorrow morning, 8am. Your favorite spot by the old oak tree."

I pause, stunned. My brain finally catches up and I turn to ask him how he knows about my favorite spot, but he's already gone, disappearing into the crowd like he was never here.

Chapter 11

Avalina

The fallen leaves crunch under my boots as I walk along the wooded trail. The autumn breeze has a bite to it today and I'm thankful for my wool coat as I clench it tighter around me and dig my hands in the ruby red pockets.

Here I'm able to escape. Surrounded by nature, the pressures of my life fade away and I can hear myself think. No longer struggling with the mask of who I used to be, wrapped up in staying on top of trends, shopping and spending money on things that mean nothing to me. No more worrying about what I don't remember and who my friends expect me to be.

Here I can simply be myself, with no filters and no mask. The tension I've been carrying eases away and I feel like I can breathe again.

I pause at a small creek burbling over rocks and sit on a fallen log. Dipping my fingers in the cool water, I'm struck by its clarity. I think of my own murky memories and how I long to recover that same sense of surety about my past.

But here, listening to the creek's quiet song, I know at least one truth still rings clear: my love for these woods, for the quiet joy of this unfettered existence.

Raising my face to the sunlight glimmering through the trees, I close my eyes and inhale the cedar and damp earth that surrounds me.

After the trip to the city that Iris and Claire planned, my missing memories have plagued me and I've felt even more disconnected from what should have been my closest friends. For not the first time, I wondered how well these friends even knew me.

Iris and Claire, I feel a bond with, because I have known them both almost my entire life. But Amanda and Jessica? I feel as close to them as I do a random stranger I meet on the street. We seem worlds apart.

My mind shifts back to the surrounding woods. For now, it's enough. It has to be.

Rising, I dust off my pants and continue down the trail, wondering when or if Kieran will show up. I pause at the edge of the clearing, taking in the unbroken expanse of sky above me. The trees fall away, opening up to a vista overlooking the valley below.

A slight movement catches my eye - a presence shifting in the shadows of the trees. I turn, scanning the woods behind me, but see nothing. I blink and that's when I see him - a tall figure emerging from the trees. As he comes closer, I recognize him. Kieran.

Kieran makes his way towards me. He moves with predatory grace, his dark gaze intent.

I'm rooted to the spot in anticipation. Even the birdsong has stilled. It's as if the entire forest is holding its breath, transfixed by this man's commanding presence.

Watching him glide towards me, I can't help but take in his tall form, dressed in the all black attire I've seen him in around town. His black hair falls slightly in his face, casting shadows on his sharp cheekbones.

He steps closer, moving to stand beside me, and leans against the tree trunk. "We used to see each other."

"In secret," he quickly adds, as he sees the furrow appear on my brow. "We met in these woods, actually".

"We did?" Shock colors my words. Why has no one mentioned this before now?

His lips curve into a sensuous smile. "Why do you think this is your favorite spot?"

He continues. "We met about eight months before your accident. We got to talking and realized we had more in common than one might think. After a few run-ins and a stern talking down from Iris to stay away from you, we kept our relationship secret."

·

My mind reels, trying to make sense of his words. "For how long?" I whisper.

"Until your accident. Until you didn't remember." He says simply.

"But that was months ago. You have said nothing until now. Why?" I demand.

He sighs and looks away, running a hand through his dark tresses. "I thought I was doing you a favor. I knew how much you wanted out. Out of this town, out of this role. I wanted you to have that without me dragging you down. I thought I was giving you what you wanted."

I cross my arms over my chest. "Prove it," I declare, staring him down with a boldness I do not feel.

Kieran simply pulls his phone out from his back pocket, typing something before turning it so I can see what's displayed.

I peer at the screen, unable to process what I'm seeing at first. Photos. Lots of photos. And video. I tap the first photo, making it larger. It's us. I glance around. The photo appears to have been taken here, in these woods. I look at the date. Ten months ago. I tap the screen and start scrolling through pictures and video of us here in these woods, by the quarry, the lake. Our arms are around each other. We're smiling at the camera. There are more images of what looks to be an old farm, where we're cuddled on a plaid blanket, kissing.

Scrolling, I find more photos of us in my apartment, last December when I had my holiday decorations up. Suddenly Kieran's hand is there on the phone, taking it away from me. I think I glimpse a bed between my fingers.

"I don't have any photos of you on my phone. For all I know, these are all fake..." my voice trails off, the disbelief clear in my argument.

"Some of these are from your phone." Kieran says as he puts his phone back in his pocket. "After your accident, after I realized you didn't remember, I deleted all evidence from your phone, email, everything."

Anger surges through me. "You deleted them? When? What gave you the right to do that?" I push against him, wanting distance.

Kieran doesn't move, doesn't even seem to register my anger. "When you were in the hospital. I asked your sister for your phone. Told her what I wanted to do. She agreed to go along with it."

"Wait," I hold out my hands. "Iris knew about us?"

He finally looks guilty at that. "She did. Not at first, but eventually you wanted to tell her. But after the accident, I wanted you to have a fresh start. Not be dragged down by my shadows." He glances at me. "You may not remember our relationship, but you've lived here your whole life, Avalina. I know you know what I do."

I shift my weight, suddenly nervous. "I know the rumors."

Kieran bites back, "And what are those rumors, Avalina?"

A shiver ghosts down my spine, but I'm not so sure it's from nerves this time or if it's from the way my name sounds on Kieran's lips.

"That your family is involved in less than savory business." I slowly make out. Kieran just stares, waiting for me to continue. "Buying off whoever you want, blackmailing those you can't."

"Is that all you've heard?"

"Iris may have mentioned to stay away from you and your family. That you're bad. That you, in particular, aren't afraid to hurt people to get what you want."

"Hmm" Kieran's voice rumbles. "Your sister is right."

"All that you've heard," Kieran begins, "is true. And whatever you think you know about how bad and dark I am, I promise I'm worse."

Mouth agape, I stare up at him, confused by the picture my words are painting in contrast to the man standing next to me. "Why are you here now, telling me this?" I peer up at him through my lashes. His chiseled jaw flexes as he stares back at me with those dark eyes.

Suddenly I'm pressed against the tree trunk, his arms caging me in. "I thought I could do the right thing. I thought I could be the hero for once. Do something good. But I'm not a hero, Avalina. I'm not a good man."

I swallow, thoughts scrambling to keep up. Iris had briefly mentioned Kieran and the Calder family to me after the accident. I knew who they were, what they supposedly did. But here Kieran was, telling me we had a secret relationship.

Would I have done that? Had a secret relationship with someone who dealt in power and money? Who bribed and extorted to get what they wanted? And even if I had done that, would I do that now?

I blink, realizing how close Kieran still is to me, how I haven't moved. I put my hands on his chest, thinking I should push him away. But somehow my hands don't get the signal, and instead of pushing, I'm grip his leather jacket with my fists, inhaling his scent of whiskey and smoke.

I exhale a shaky breath and force my hands to my side.

"This... is a lot to take in."

"I know." Kieran steps back, sensing I need space.

"I don't know..." my voice trails off.

"I know." Kieran says again. He pulls his phone from his pocket, typing once again.

A ding rings out in the silence. I look at my phone, seeing the text from an unknown number with a link that says, *Here's everything.*

"It's from me," Kieran states.

I click the link and can only blink as I watch my phone download photos, videos, texts, and emails. All from Kieran. To Kieran. With Kieran.

"It's everything I deleted. I figured you'd want it back. If you don't, just delete it."

I'm out of words. My brain has shut off, overwhelmed by the information. I just stare at my phone, startled as Kieran's hand touches my cheek, pushing some hair away from my face and behind my ear. His touch ignited an inferno within me, reducing my trepidation to ash.

"I should go," he murmurs.

Then he turns, his strides quickly putting distance between us.

"Wait!" I call out, desperate and confused. But he's already walking away, soon disappearing into the shadows of the woods.

I stand alone, my heart racing, my mind spinning as I try to make sense of what just happened.

Only moments ago, I was reveling in the simple joys of nature, content in my solitude. Now everything feels different. Charged. Alive.

My fingers drift to my cheek, chasing the phantom caress of his hand. Kieran. A complete stranger, yet somehow, there is a magnetic pull I don't understand. Now curiosity burns within me, an insatiable need to unravel the mystery of this dark, intense man. What is this connection between us?

As the rising sun causes the sky to turn from golden pink to bright blue, I pause, realizing I've been here much longer than planned. I need answers and I think I know who may have them.

Chapter 12

Avalina

I arrive at my sister's house, a modest brick home tucked away in a quiet suburban neighborhood. I knock sharply on the vibrant red door, adorned with a wreath of dried flowers. The door swings open, revealing my sister's smiling face, framed by the colorful fall leaves that cover the front yard. Surprise spread across her features as she greets me into her cozy abode.

"Avalina? What are you doing here so late?"

I step inside. "I need to ask you something."

She studies me for a moment before nodding slowly. We sit at the kitchen table.

"What do you know about Kieran Calder?" I ask without preamble.

My sister frowns, hesitation in her eyes. "Why the sudden interest? Have you remembered something?"

"I just... I need to know what you know. It's hard to explain."

She sighs. "Avalina, perhaps it best if you leave the past in the past."

"Please," I implore my sister. "Tell me everything you know."

She looks uneasy but continues. "You and Kieran... you had a relationship before the accident."

"You knew about this? And you didn't tell me?" I exclaim, rage rising to the surface. I back away from Iris, needing to put distance between us.

"I'm sorry, Avie!" Iris wails, as she moves to follow me. "I never liked your relationship with Kieran, sneaking around and trying to hide it from everyone. You know what they say about the Calder family, you know what he does. Is that really someone you want to be with?" Iris pleads. "He's dangerous, Avie."

"Better than boring, better than living a lie." I reply, fury sharpening my tongue. How dare she keep this from me? And then act like she did it to protect me?

"Why go through all the trouble of showing me pictures and videos, trying to 'help me get my memory back' when the whole time you were *keeping* memories from me? Who are you to decide what memories I'm allowed to have?" I'm shouting now, my words honed blades designed to fly true.

Iris' face falls. I feel like I *should* feel guilty, but mostly I feel free. Having this out in the open, knowing what Kieran has told me is true, I feel a weight lifting off my chest. I look away, letting the silence grow.

I will not apologize for my words, not when Iris has been trying to get me to go back to my old life this entire time, when all I wanted was to break free.

"How did you find out?" Iris whispers, the silence too loud to speak.

"Kieran told me," I reply, my words short. "When did I tell you? About him, I mean."

"You told me after you were with him for a few months. Swore me to secrecy."

"Did Mom and Dad know?"

"About Kieran? No way. You know how they are. They wouldn't approve."

She's right. Our parents are all about the appearance one presents to the world, and dating a mafia boss wouldn't fit their image.

"I stand by what I said, Avalina," Iris tells me. I know she's serious when she uses my full name. "Be sure about Kieran. His life is dangerous, and he'll just bring that danger to you."

I nod slowly, taking in my sister's ominous words, trying to feign nonchalance when I feel like anger is going to boil me from the inside out.

She clasps my hand, concern in her eyes. "Be careful, Avalina. Some things are better left in the past."

Iris tries to hold my hand, but I pull back, my eyes narrowing. "Will you just stop already?" I hiss, the volume of my words rising as the storm inside of me builds. "You think you're protecting me, but all you're doing is suffocating me!"

My feet are moving before my mind does, and the echo of the slamming door rings behind me as I burst outside, my breath coming in angry gasps. Iris's pleading voice still rings in my ears, pressing me to go let Kieran go. As soon as I'm outside, I get into my car and head home.

I don't get far before overwhelm is threading its vines around me and wrapping tight.

I debate driving to Claire's apartment, but I would have to drive over the bridge by Lockwood Lake and I haven't driven there since the accident. Anytime I've tried, I break out in a cold sweat and my heart races. My therapist suggested I try exposure therapy to see if that would help me get over my fear of the bridge, but so far I've just been avoiding it completely, too terrified of the waves of panic and nausea that come with it.

A frustrated hiss rushes past my lips as I resign myself towards my original destination, arriving at my apartment on autopilot, too consumed by the hot swell of anger and betrayal.

One thing I hated about my life growing up was I felt like choices were taken away from me. That my parents predetermined my path based on how much money we had and how much more they wanted. My looks, friends, hobbies, and education had all swirled around the golden road laid out before me, when all I had wanted was to wander the wooded trail instead.

And if Kieran knew me, he would have known this. Yet he still kept our relationship a secret from me, getting rid of any evidence that we had a relationship. And my sister went right along with it.

I was so tired of others deciding for me, trying to control the path my life took.

Walking through my apartment door, I text Claire.

> Did you know I was with Kieran Calder before the accident?

> What??? What are you talking about??

Before I can type out the next message, my phone is ringing, the noise loud in my quiet space. I'm not surprised to see Claire's name flash on the screen.

Pressing the screen, I don't even bother with a hello. "Did you know?"

"What? This is a joke, right? You and Kieran Calder? You would have told me!"

I let my head fall into my hands, unsure of what to say. I thought I would have told Claire. I suppose I'm glad I didn't, because this means she isn't another person who lied and hid something from me. But I also don't want to reveal something that will hurt her because I kept a secret from her.

"Avie?" Claire sounds unsure. "What's going on?"

"Can you... can you come over? I need to show you something. I'll explain everything."

"Of course, I'll be right there."

I spend the time waiting for Claire by straightening up and cleaning things that don't need to be cleaned. I just need to move, to release this frantic crawling under my skin that feels like it's going to eat me alive.

I practically run to the door when I hear the knock, opening it as Claire rushes inside, eyes wide.

"Okay, spill. Were you and Kieran together? And you didn't tell me?" Anger swells in her voice at the last part, but I know it's because she's hurt. So am I. Everything feels bruised inside.

I walk over to my couch and flop down, groaning. "I don't even know where to begin. The past day has been a lot." Claire follows me and sits down, tossing her purse and keys on my wooden coffee table.

"Were you and Kieran together?"

"It appears so." I hold up my hands in apology before the questions I can see blooming on her face can begin. "I don't remember it. The only reason I know is because Kieran told me, backed it up with all the deleted pictures off my phone, and I guess Iris knew because she confirmed it."

Claire's eyes grow so wide they're practically overtaking her face. "Hold up. He *deleted* photos from your phone? Who does that? And your sister knew and said nothing?"

I throw my hands up. "Oh, I know! I told you the past day has been intense. I'm still trying to piece everything together myself."

I tell Claire about the past day, up to when I left my sister's house and texted her. That's when she gets up from the couch.

"Where are you going?"

"To get ice cream. This amount of drama calls for ice cream."

I can't fault her logic.

She calls over to me from my kitchen. "What do you want, chocolate chip cookie dough or brownie batter?"

"Cookie dough." I holler back.

Claire makes her way back over, pints of ice cream and spoons in hand. She settles down before holding her hand out to me expectantly.

"Let me see your phone."

"My phone?"

"Yeah, you said Kieran gave you back all the pictures and video he deleted. I want to see them."

"You're right, this totally needs ice cream." I say as I hand the phone over and take the cookie dough ice cream from her.

A couple of hours later, pizza and wine joined the ice cream. We've been through everything repeatedly, and I'm still not sure how I feel about any of it.

I toss my head back on the arm of the couch and stare at the ceiling. "I just don't know what to think about any of this."

"I do." Claire responds.

"You do?" I look over to where Claire is petting Conan, who is curled up in her lap.

"Yes, angry! But also, it's kind of romantic. I mean, you wanted your relationship with Kieran to be a secret, or else I would have known about it." She narrows her eyes. "Right?"

I nod fervently. "Of course, yes."

"And we all know his family is into shady business, so I can see where he thought he was protecting you. But now, he misses you and wants you back, I think."

"This would be simpler if I could remember any of it."

"Yeah, it would."

"There are rumors…" Claire begins.

Leaning in closer to her, I ask, "What kind of rumors?"

"That the Calders, well at least Kieran and his brother, Liam, are actually trying to do good for the city. That they're trying to clean things up after their father died."

"Clean things up?"

"Less money through drugs and blackmail and more money through investing, I guess. Anyway, it's just what I heard."

There's silence for a moment, then Claire asks, "Do you think you're going to date him?"

"I don't know. A part of me wants to, but it's strange, having him remember me, but I can't remember him."

"Just start over."

"Just like that?"

"Yep, just like that."

I'm still pondering Claire's words as I get ready for bed later that night. There's something about him that draws me in, but I'm not sure if I'm prey for his web, or if what I see in him is just another version of myself. A creature wanting to break free of the chains placed upon us at birth, wanting to escape and fly away, to get away from the expectations of everyone around us.

Before I can think too much about it, I grab my phone and send a text to Kieran.

> Why were we together? We're from two separate worlds.

He doesn't respond right away, and I debate putting my phone on the other side of the room so I can't chicken out and unsend the text.

I've just closed my eyes when I hear the ding.

> *We were both born in cages we wanted to destroy.*

I stare at the words on the screen until the moon rises high in the sky, casting its glow through my window and illuminating all my shadows.

Chapter 13

Avalina

I need more coffee. I was up way too late last night, combing through everything Kieran sent me. I'm still in shock and my mind keeps replaying all the conversations I've had in the past couple of weeks about Kieran and the Calders as I shelve books at the library.

Anger simmers just under the surface as I remember that Iris knew this whole time.

She *knew*.

And didn't say a word to me.

It makes me wonder if I can trust my sister. What other secrets is she keeping from me?

"Avie!"

I jump in surprise, startled as Mavis lets out a roar of laughter down the row, tossing her brunette curls. "I've been calling your name over and over, but you were lost to the world. Who is it?"

I shake my head in confusion. "Who is who?"

Her nose wrinkles as she grins. "Oh, come on, I know that look. You're thinking about someone." She sing-songs this last part.

"Oh, no, I am not." I protest, but I know the blush rising to my cheeks is giving me away.

Mavis snorts, patting me on the shoulder with a gleam in her eye. "If you say so." She straightens. "I was coming to find you because I was going to go grab some lunch from Jo's. They make the best bacon sandwich, and I could literally kill someone for one right now."

It's my turn to laugh. Mavis is a kindhearted woman, and I can't imagine her being violent towards anyone. "Sure, that'd be great. You know, a BLT sounds good. Just make sure it's with their sourdough bread."

Mavis interrupts me. "Oh, yes. That sourdough bread is to die for."

While Mavis goes to grab our lunch, I move back towards the circulation desk, ready to help any patrons. It's a quiet day, so I pull my phone out of my pocket to quickly check what I've missed. I keep my phone on silent at work, so there's always a phone call or text to respond to.

I'm scrolling through, sending brief replies where I can and deleting the spam when my breath lodges in my throat. It's a text. From Kieran.

I shove my phone back in my pocket so abruptly I almost lose my balance. I take a breath. Shake my head. Pull my phone back out of my pocket. Sigh as I shove it back in again.

"Come on, Avalina, just look at it." I tell myself. Glancing around to make sure the library is clear, I press a shaky finger to the screen to open up the message.

> *Are you okay?*

I blink. That was not what I was expecting. And also something I hadn't asked myself. *Was I okay?* I don't let myself think about it too hard before I quickly type back.

> *I'm not sure. It's all a bit overwhelming.*

> *Would it help to talk? Or would you rather I stay away?*

I take my time before I respond, unsure of what would actually help. In the end I decide talking would be best.

> *I think talking would help.*

We quickly make a plan to meet after work. Kieran suggests he can bring some Chinese takeout over for dinner, and we'll talk. Part of me feels like I should feel uncertain, cautious even. I don't even really know Kieran.

But I can't deny that I feel soothed by his presence. With Kieran, I can let the mask fall away and just be myself. Even in the short time I've spent with him, at least since the accident, I know that much.

Chapter 14

Kieran

The underbelly of the city is never quiet, but tonight it hums with a particular kind of urgency that set my instincts ablaze. The docks, usually lost in shadows and elusive dealings, bristles with tension as Liam and I make our way through the maze of containers. Finn's words were a pulse in my veins — his father, Sean O'Neil, was up to something.

"Keep your eyes peeled," I murmur to Liam, my voice barely louder than the lapping water against the piers. Our steps are soundless, a dance we'd perfected over countless nights like this, chasing whispers and confronting threats head-on.

"Always do, big brother," Liam replies, his tone light but his gaze sharp as he scans the area.

The moon hangs low, a silent witness, painting the metal giants around us in silver strokes. We move like specters, our presence nothing but a mere suggestion to the untrained eye. Yet, despite our stealth, there is an unmistakable electricity in the air, a buzz that whispers of imminent danger, of secrets clawing their way to the surface.

We arrive at the docks, and instantly I know. More men than usual loiter, their stances too casual to be anything but forced. They are Sean's guys; I'd recognize their brand of menace anywhere. And the security — tighter than a snare drum — sings a clear message: Sean O'Neil is fortifying his fortress.

"Something's not right," Liam breathes out, his blue eyes reflecting the unease taking root in my chest.

"Agreed." My gaze sweeps over the figures that skulk near the water's edge, each man a sentinel to whatever dark secret was cocooned within those containers.

Liam leans closer, his warmth a fleeting comfort in the chill of the night. "There are more of them than there should be. He's expecting trouble or... starting it."

"Or both," I reply, the taste of coming confrontation bitter on my tongue. I can feel the thrum of my own blood, a rhythm that demands action, that longs for the sweet release of conflict resolved by the might of my own hands.

But patience — a virtue I'd cultivated amidst the chaos of leadership — holds me taut like a bowstring. We need to know what Sean is guarding so fiercely before we step into the light and reveal ourselves. It is a game of shadows, and we play it well.

"Let's find out what he's hiding," I propose, my voice a velvet promise of retribution. With a nod, Liam and I press deeper into the maze of containers, the scent of brine chasing us, along with the electric anticipation of a storm on the horizon.

Liam and I move with purpose, our footsteps silent on the damp cobblestone, our shadows fleeting phantoms in the dim glow of the harbor lights.

"Sean's sweating," Liam murmurs, his voice a low thrum that matches the distant hum of a cargo ship. "All this interference... It's got him rattled."

I nod, my jaw clenched. The intel from Finn and Sloane has been a thorn in their father's side, a constant agitation that I know is driving Sean toward desperation. He isn't a man who tolerates insubordination or uncertainty. And we've served up a generous helping of both.

"Good," I said, the word slicing through the cool air. "Let him feel the heat. Let him make mistakes."

Liam's chuckle is a soft ripple in the quiet. "Careful, brother. You almost sound like you're enjoying this."

"Perhaps I am," I admit, though the truth was more complex. This game we play is dangerous, a dance on the edge of a knife that can cut deep if we stumble, even worse it can cut those we care about. But the thrill of the hunt, the allure of unraveling Sean's machinations—it ignites something primal within me.

We trail a pair of men, burly silhouettes that cut through the fog like ships setting course through treacherous waters. They lead us to a warehouse, its rusted exterior a testament to years of neglect. The hushed tones of conversation reach us, and we press ourselves against the cold metal of the storage container adjacent to the building, ears straining to capture the fragments of dialogue seeping through the thin walls.

"Tonight's shipment... critical," one voice rasps, the words punctuated by the clink of what can only be weaponry being handled.

"Boss is clear about it—no screw-ups," another replies, the menace in his tone unmistakable. "He says Calder's been a real pain in the ass. Wants this done smooth, no hitches."

"Calder..." The name hung in the air, a ghostly presence that hovers between us and them. I am that name, a whisper of dread in the underbelly of the city, a ghost in Sean's grand plans.

A surge of satisfaction courses through me, hot and heady as the finest whiskey. We are affecting him, disrupting the order he so desperately clings to. And here, in the pitch-black recesses of the docks, I feel the power of that influence like a living thing.

My muscles tense and my heart thunders like a relentless drumbeat against my ribs. I edge closer to the threshold of the warehouse. Shadows dance under the flickering lights, and the air was thick with the brine of the sea and oil—a stark contrast to the scent of jasmine and sandalwood that always clings to Avalina's skin, a reminder of a world far removed from this darkness.

"Kieran," Liam hisses, a warning etched into that single word. He grips my arm, the pressure of his fingers biting into flesh. "Wait."

I grit my teeth, every fiber of my being screaming for action. The urge to storm in, to disrupt whatever vile trade Sean is orchestrating within those walls, is a siren call luring me toward recklessness.

"Damn it, Liam, we can't just stand here!" My voice is a low growl, barely containing the fury lacing each syllable. "We've got him cornered, spooked. Now's the time to strike."

"Think, brother." Liam's tone is a cool balm to my heated rage. "We don't know what he's planning, or who else is involved."

"Since when are you the voice of reason?" Despite the sarcasm, I know he speaks sense. Our past confrontations have taught us both the price of impulsiveness—bruises that run far deeper than skin, wounds that never quite heal.

"Since I started listening to Sloane's advice, and not just admiring her... other qualities." A wry smile plays across his lips, a fleeting distraction from our grim setting.

I allow myself a moment, a brief chuckle at his expense, before refocusing on the task at hand. "Fine," I concede, though the words taste like ash on my tongue.

"Good. Let's backtrack, find a better vantage point. We gather intel, understand the full scope. Then, when we're ready..." Liam trails off, his gaze hardening, the blue of his eyes turning to steel.

"Then we burn it all down," I finish for him, the promise hanging heavy in the night air.

We retreat into the shadows, moving with the silent precision of predators. In the quiet that follows, my thoughts wander to Avalina again—her fierce spirit, the curve of her body beneath my hands. Desire flares, a welcome heat amidst the cold calculation of our mission. It is a craving as raw and undeniable as the thirst for vengeance.

"Patience," Liam murmurs again, picking up on my nerves but not understanding their source.

"Patience," I agree, the word a vow, a whispered caress, a smoldering ember awaiting the spark to ignite an inferno.

Chapter 15

Avalina

I find Kieran leaning by the wall to my apartment after work. His dark gaze pierces my soul, ripping away the carefully constructed lies I wrap around myself in order to sleep in peace. He turns, eyes flashing as they meet mine. I approach slowly, heart pounding.

"I brought your favorite, egg rolls with honey," he says as he holds up a bag filled with takeout containers.

I lift my chin. "What if it's changed?" I challenge, despite the knowledge that he is right.

He just shrugs. "Then I'll get something else."

Kieran follows me into the apartment, immediately going to pull out plates and silverwear. It takes me back for a moment until I realize that he's been here before. Lots of times. I have the photos and video to prove it.

I cross the small space to the kitchen, slipping off my shoes and setting my bag down on the counter before sitting on one of the stools by the counter. I'm mesmerized as I watch Kieran move effortlessly around my space, setting up the containers and plates in front of me and then moving to get my favorite tea from the fridge.

Conan waltzes into the kitchen, weaving through Kieran's legs as he moves about the space. I'm about to call Conan away when Kieran reaches down and gives my tabby cat scratches behind his ear, his favorite spot.

"Don't worry, Conan, I didn't forget about you," Kieran says as he pulls some grilled chicken from a box, tearing it into pieces before putting it into Conan's bowl.

I try to shift away from the discomfort of watching someone know me so obviously well when I don't know them at all. Kieran finishes setting things up and then comes to sit beside me, piling his plate high with chow mein. I grab some egg rolls and we simply eat in silence as my mind tries to catch up with what is happening.

This differs from how it is with Claire or any of my friends. There's no pretense here, no need to force a conversation or adhere to a predetermined set of topics. Here I can just be me.

I finally give in. "I don't know what to do."

At first Kieran is silent, assessing. Then he tilts his head, looking over at me before saying, "Honestly, I don't either."

"What do you mean?"

"I thought I should stay away. Your memory loss offered a clean break. Sure, I remembered everything, but you didn't. You could move on, have a life free of my darkness."

"But how do you know I didn't want a life with you?" I question.

"We kept our relationship a secret for a reason." Kieran sighs, running a hand through his hair. "My life. It's not completely safe. I didn't want to bring you into that."

"But you wanted to make it safer, right? That's what you're doing with Liam and Finn?" I ask.

"That's the hope. But who knows when that will happen."

"What's stopping you?"

"Sean O'Neil. He's not a fan of going legit. He prefers money and power."

I hum around a pork dumpling like I know what he's talking about. I mean, I kind of do. That's why Amanda and Jessica, even Iris and Claire to some extent, like the parties and shopping and travel. It's all about money and power. They want more, while I want just enough to live my life.

"It feels like I don't know you at all," I whisper, looking down at my now empty plate. As Kieran shifts, I feel his hands on my seat, turning me towards him on the stool. I bite my lip and glance up, nerves racing through me. "I'm sorry," I begin.

"No." Kieran says. "I told you, Avalina, you have nothing to be sorry for."

"I just..." I begin, but don't know what to say, lifting my hands up in exasperation.

"Green." Kieran says.

"What?" I ask, confused and slightly alarmed.

"My favorite color is green."

"Oh." I blink.

"I like to read, but mostly stick to history and mythology."

I just nod.

"I hate the snow."

"I'm so sorry you live here, then." I chuckle.

Kieran smirks. "What else do you want to know?"

I look Kieran fully in the eyes now. "Everything."

"Tell me about yourself," I say softly. "What do you *really* do?"

Kieran's lips form a hard line, all playful banter gone. His gaze turned serious, distant. "I'm the head of my family, the Calders. We're one of the most powerful families in the country, with business interests in many sectors."

"Like a mafia family?" I ask, only half joking. I know the rumors.

Kieran's smile fades. "Not exactly, though we do engage in some... extra-legal activities at times to protect our interests." His eyes meet mine. "My role comes with a great deal of power, but also responsibility and danger. There are many who would see my family destroyed."

I swallow hard, a frisson of fear running down my spine.

"Does that frighten you?" Kieran asks softly. "Now that you know the truth about me?"

I hesitate, torn between my attraction to Kieran and the peril that comes with him. "I don't know," I admit. "It frightens me, but also intrigues me." I reach out to brush my fingers along his jaw. "Everyone has told me to stay away from you, that you're dangerous. But there's more to you than meets the eye, isn't there?"

Kieran turns his head to press a kiss to my palm, his eyes never leaving mine. "Just as there is more to you, Avalina Hartwell, than your serene facade suggests."

My breath catches at the intensity in his gaze. At that moment, I realize Kieran understands me in a way no one else does. He sees beyond the surface to the hidden depths within.

And I realize, despite the danger, I can't walk away from him now. I am already falling, tumbling into the abyss of my desire for this complicated, enigmatic man.

We spend the next hours talking about everything, and while I understand Kieran already probably knows everything about me, he doesn't interrupt me or say anything as I respond to his answers with answers of my own.

Our favorite animals, places to visit, food to eat, hobbies. Any random fact or question I can ask Kieran, I do. And he answers every single one. I can't deny I feel comfortable in Kieran's presence. Even Conan is relaxed around him.

We're currently on the couch and I'm sitting close to Kieran, with Conan curled up on Kieran's lap. We're watching the latest episode of my favorite baking show and I'm drooling over the cookies, or biscuits as they're calling them on the television. One contestant is currently making butter cookies and I can't help the appreciative hum I make.

Kieran slides a glance in my direction. "I'll go buy you all the butter cookies in the world if they cause you to make noises like that."

I laugh and playfully slap his arm. He's been doing this all night, throwing barely veiled flirtatious comments in my direction. Most of the time I laugh it off or veer the topic elsewhere, but the more he does it, the more confident I feel.

"I guess I know what you'll be doing tomorrow, then." I smirk.

Kieran barks out a laugh, startling Conan to jump off his lap and throw a scowl in our direction. I don't think I've heard him laugh before. The need to hear him laugh again crawls its way into my chest, making a home for itself.

Kieran turns back to the television, and I can't resist the opportunity to drink my fill of his strong jaw and black lashes.

Even with all the evidence Kieran gave me, the videos and photos to help fill in the gaps in my memories, it still doesn't feel real having him next to me, so relaxed and at ease. I keep waiting for the other shoe to drop. I just can't shake the feeling that there's something around the corner, something that neither of us can see, but it's stalking us all the same.

We continue watching the show, sitting side by side. Eventually I notice Kieran's hand a hairsbreadth from mine. As the episode continues and the contestants move on to a technical baking challenge involving caramelized white chocolate, Kieran's thumb brushes against my pinkie.

Ever so gently, he caresses my finger, each soft sweep sending a jolt through me. I try to focus on the bakers and their sudden hatred for white chocolate, but my entire world is narrowing down to the feeling of Kieran's skin on mine. How can this man I can't remember feel like the soft embrace of home?

Heat flares between us, as taught as a bowstring, and I resist the urge to rub my thighs together to soothe the ache that is quickly building between my legs. My mind is screaming at me, telling me I don't know this man who sparks such intense desire with just a glance in my direction, but I feel pulled to him in a way I can't explain.

I feel like a fish on dry land, gasping for words to explain the turmoil I'm feeling. "I just wish I could remember..." I trail off. Kieran says nothing, but his eyes speak volumes. "I know I have the emails and pictures and everything else, but..."

"It's not the same as remembering." Kieran finishes for me. "I understand. Honestly, Lina, I have no idea if your memories will come back or not. Of course, I hope they do. I'd love for you to remember. But I'm a realist. I'll understand if they don't. I'll just make new ones with you now." His lips quirk up at this last part, a smirk gracing his features that twists my insides and sends heat swirling to my core.

Kieran may remember me, but I only have a handful of interactions with him, and this flirting feels out of my element. I try to think of another topic to switch to when it dawns on me. "Wait, what did you call me?"

A furrow forms across Kieran's brow and the corner of his whiskey-colored eyes crinkle. "What do you mean? Lina?"

"Yes, no one calls me that."

"I do," he rumbles. "Does it bother you?"

I stop and think. "No, I like it." I smile at him. "Do you know what caused my accident? No one seems to know."

"No, I looked into it and have been following leads, but they all dried up. I've got someone looking into it again."

"What kind of leads?"

Kieran turns towards me. "It wasn't an accident, Lina. Your break lines were cut."

"Wait, so *someone* caused my accident?" Alarm barrels through me. Until now, the theory was that something must have startled me, like a deer, since the doctors ruled out all medication conditions that might have caused the accident.

"It appears so. Don't worry, I'll find out who did it. I'll make them pay." Kieran grows this last part out.

I lick my lips at his statement, a movement Kieran's eyes catch and immediately snag on. My breath hitches as every inch of my body is aware with startling clarity how close Kieran is to me. I can't help but wonder what it was about Kieran's anger that feels like a warm embrace instead of a threat, why his fierce need to protect me has warmth spreading across my body.

It was while contemplating the intelligence of my body when Kieran moves as quick as lightning, caging me against the couch with his powerful arms.

"Tell me to stop and I will, Lina," he whispers before bending head to my shoulder, my neck automatically tilting to give him more space.

A rumble escapes him as he gently kisses the spot below my ear, catching my breath as easily as he catches my earlobe between his teeth, gently licking and nibbling.

My hands wrap around him, pulling him to me as he moves to claim my lips, his eyes darkening like the night sky. My mind races with the sudden knowledge that this was what I have been craving. This is what I have been looking for.

Amanda set me up with Mickey James, who tried to be charming, but completely failed. I wanted honest and upfront, so I felt protected and safe. I wanted to be seen for who I was and not the image someone else wanted me to play pretend at being.

It feels surreal until I realize that, unlike me, Kieran had never forgotten. While I can't remember our time from before the accident, Kieran does, and the images he shared with me confirm that.

With his broad frame encircling me, I can feel the power and control emanating from him. As his knee found its place between my thighs and his grip on my hip and neck tightened, I'm reminded that yes, Kieran knows exactly what I want.

I melt against him, spurred by the knowledge that I don't have to hide from him. His lips nip at mine and pleasure surges through me.

I moan, hands trailing up his back to grip at his hair, holding him still while I arch into him.

"Fuck," he groans, and his hand sweep up my hip and around my breast, gently squeezing and teasing my nipple through my top. His hand moves to the back of the couch, while his gaze snares mine, igniting a blaze within me as he ever so slowly shifts his weight forward, his knee pressing more into my core.

Lightning zings through me, shoving every thought out of my mind. The only thing I know is his taste, his smell, his weight pressing against me, swirling my desire even higher.

Every part of my awareness narrows to where Kieran's body meets mine, to the pleasure humming in my blood, the teasing touches, and slow glides of Kieran's palm on my skin as I chase that rapture almost within reach. Tossing my head back, I grab onto that wave of euphoria, muscles clenching in delicious agony as electricity crackles through my veins.

I come down from my high in a delicious haze, my limbs heavy and liquid. Kieran shifts, pulling me to straddle his lap, and I wind my hands behind his neck, pulling him into me for a kiss when his phone rings, interrupting us.

Kieran mumbles something that sounds very much like a growl as he pulls his phone out of his pocket and glances at it. "It's my brother. I have to answer it. He'd text if it wasn't important." He said the last bit with a frown on his face, the apology clear in his eyes and he pressed the screen with a biting, "What is it?".

I can't hear Liam on the other end, but I know from the way Kieran tightens against me and clenches his jaw that whatever Liam had to say isn't good.

I try to shift myself off of Kieran's lap, but his free arm snakes around me like a steel band, keeping me solidly in place. He hangs up with a curse, shoving his phone back in his pocket like it is the one that offended him.

"I take it that our date is over?" I ask, unable to keep the disappointment out of my voice.

A grin lights up Kieran's face at that. I catch myself thinking I'd do anything to keep that smile there. "A date, is it?"

"Well, what else would you call it? You brought dinner."

"But now our date is being interrupted." He frowns and looks at me through his lashes.

"I'll see you later?"

"Always." He leans over, pressing a kiss to my forehead before seeing himself out of my apartment.

Chapter 16

Kieran

Everyone thinks I wear black because I want to seem menacing and powerful. It's really because it hides the blood.

My black shirt and jeans are currently free of blood, but you never know what the night is going to hold. The warehouse room I'm in is dusty, with the last rays of daylight filtering through cracked windows, casting long shadows on the grimy concrete floor. The air hangs heavy with the scent of old motor oil and damp cardboard boxes stacked haphazardly in one corner. Rusty metal shelves line the walls, cluttered with tools and spare parts.

In the center of the room, a weathered wooden table stands, its surface marred by years of use and bearing scars from countless discussions like the one taking place now. Liam is fidgeting in his chair across from me, restless to be moving and not sitting here planning. I don't blame him.

I sigh. We learned from Rocco that Sean is expecting a shipment of trafficked people tonight, and he plans on using them to staff his various establishments.

I know families like mine often built their foundation on illegal activities like trafficking. But that doesn't mean I have to tolerate it now. My blood boils and I wish there was a face for me to pummel.

"We need to be careful," I say. "We can't let anyone know what we're planning." My eyes flick to Liam, who nods in agreement, his fingers running through his light brown hair, a nervous habit that never seems to leave him, even when he is in control.

"We'll have to be strategic about this." He leans forward, his elbows resting on the table as he studies the blueprints spread out before us. "Finn, you've got the inside scoop. How many guards are involved?"

Finn's low voice is gravelly as he speaks. "There are usually two at the entrance, but they can be easily taken care of." He glances over at me, and I nod. "The real problem will be inside..."

A soft knock on the door causes my heart to leap into my throat. I'm not the only one affected, as Finn and Liam have both stilled, our hands on our guns. The door creaks open to reveal Slone, dressed head to toe in night black tactical gear.

"Sloane, what are you doing here?" Finn pushes up from the table, lumbering over to his sister.

"It's not safe for you here."

"Oh, shut it, Finn and hand me a rifle."

I smirk as I toss Sloane a rifle from the table. Finn looks murderous while Liam is staring with hearts in his eyes as Sloane checks the gun out.

Finn's voice rolls like thunder, "Again, Sloane, why are you here?"

"Because I'm the best shot out of all of you and you need someone to watch your back."

"I do not need..." Finn begins, his face reddening.

Sloane just rolls her eyes and cuts her brother off, "We don't have time for this, we need to go."

"Agreed." I nod. "She's an asset, Finn. Get with the program."

The cold night air bites at my skin as we approach the nondescript warehouse, a shadow against the even darker sky. I can feel the weight of the situation pressing down on me like a physical force. Liam's tense presence to my right is a silent testament to the gravity of what we're about to do.

Finn leads the way, his muscular form barely visible in the dim light, with Liam and I flanking him like shadows tethered to his purpose.

"Remember, Sloane's got eyes on us," Finn whispers gruffly, his red hair like a beacon in the moonlight. He glances up at the rooftop where Sloane, ever the protector despite her father's archaic views, lies in wait with her rifle.

We move closer, our steps barely making a sound on the rough concrete. My heart thrums in my chest, a rhythmic drumming that echoes the danger and the adrenaline coursing through my veins.

Finn pauses, his hand going up, and we halt in unison. My heart pounds against my ribs, a relentless drum urging us forward.

"Shit, there they are," Liam hisses, his blue eyes sharp under the faint light of a distant streetlamp.

Through a crack in the warehouse door, I see it—the stark reality of Sean O'Neil's empire. Men, little more than shadows themselves, shuffle girls onto a truck like cattle to slaughter. Anger flares within me, hot and potent. These women and girls deserve freedom, not a life in chains.

"We have to stop that truck," I murmur, feeling the familiar burn of responsibility ignite within me. Avalina's face flashes in my mind, her independence and fire fueling my resolve. She wouldn't stand for this; neither will I.

Finn nods, his muscular frame tensed for action. "We move on three," Finn whispers, the ghosts of countless past transgressions etched into the lines of his face. He is more than Sean's son tonight; he is a savior in the making, a man hell-bent on retribution.

The count tickled my ears, and we surged forward as one. We had to stop that truck, liberate the innocents before they vanished into the night, swallowed by a world that would consume them whole. Every muscle in my body tensed, ready for the conflict ahead.

And so we advanced, silent avengers beneath the cloak of night, driven by a singular, burning purpose—to save those who could not save themselves.

With purpose, we edge toward the men, our movements calculated and silent. I feel the heat of the moment, the significance of our mission. This isn't just another skirmish—it's a chance to save lives, to make a difference.

Gunfire erupts, shattering the night's deceptive calm. My heart slams against my ribs, a relentless drumbeat urging me forward. Each shot fired is a declaration of war against the darkness we've sworn to eradicate. Finn moves with deadly precision, his body a weapon honed for vengeance and justice.

"Left side!" Liam shouts, his voice a sharp blade cutting through the chaos.

I pivot, sighting down the barrel of my gun, and squeeze the trigger. A man collapses, his silhouette crumpling like a marionette with its strings severed. Beside me, Liam's breaths are ragged but determined, punctuated by the steady cadence of his own shots.

"Sniper in position," Sloane's voice crackles in my earpiece, cool and detached, but I can hear the undercurrent of adrenaline. She's perched somewhere above, our guardian angel cloaked in shadows. With each precise pull of the trigger, she carves a path of safety through the treachery that seeks to swallow us whole.

Another round sends a spray of concrete dust into the air, stinging my eyes. For a moment, the world narrows to the burn of my lungs and the heat of the blood racing beneath my skin.

"Truck's clear!" Liam yells, satisfaction laced with the dark edge of anger. We've halted one monster tonight, but the beast has many heads.

Suddenly, the scent of smoke claws at my nostrils, a toxic promise spreading faster than fear. An ember of dread kindles in my gut as my gaze snaps to the warehouse, where shadows dance with a new, orange ferocity.

"Fire!" The word tastes of ash as it leaves my lips.

One of Sean's men has slipped past our barrage, a wraith set on destruction. I watch, helpless, as flames lick the sides of the building, greedily devouring the old timber.

"Damn it!" Liam curses, his voice mirroring the helplessness that threatens to engulf us.

In the distance, the blaze catches Sloane's attention. Her perch gives her a vantage point on the inferno, a guardian angel with a rifle and a heart forged in the crucible of her father's disdain.

"Girls are still inside the warehouse," she says, the words heavy with a grim determination.

We exchange glances, silent vows passing between us. These women and girls won't be left to the mercy of the flames. Not while we draw breath, not while we can still fight.

"Let's go!" Finn roars, and we charge toward the conflagration, our steps echoing with the weight of every soul we're racing to save.

Heat buffets us as we breach the warehouse door, a beastly furnace roaring to life in the bowels of the building. My lungs scream against the smoke, but I force my legs forward, Finn and Liam at my side. The blaze has already begun its ravenous dance, flickering tongues licking up towards the rafters, an inferno threatening to consume everything in its path.

"Upstairs!" I yell over the roar, pointing to where steel cages glint through the haze. Our footsteps pound on the concrete, a desperate rhythm beneath the crackle and pop of fire feasting on wood and old paint.

We burst onto the second floor, where the heat intensifies. The air is a wall of fire, nearly solid in its intensity. Girls huddle together, eyes wide with terror behind the bars. Their cries are muffled by the cacophony of destruction all around us.

"Stand back!" Finn bellows, his voice a command forged in the furnace of chaos. He slams his body against the lock, once, twice, breaking it open. As the girls flood out, coughing and stumbling, Liam guides them towards the stairs, his charm now a lifeline in the form of calm directions and promises of safety.

I move to the next cage, heat searing my skin through my shirt, sweat and soot mingling on my brow. I grasp the padlock, heat biting into my flesh, but I don't relent. With a grunt, I wrench it free, ignoring the blistering pain that tells me I'll bear this night's mark for a long time.

"Go, go, go!" I urge, and they do, scrambling past me like frightened deer. But there's another cage, and my heart sinks when I see it. Time is a luxury we no longer have; the fire is a greedy thing, enveloping everything with indiscriminate hunger.

"Kieran, we've got to move!" Liam shouts, panic edging his voice for the first time.

"More here!" I call back, unwilling to leave anyone to this fiery tomb. My hands tremble as I fight another lock. It gives way, and I shepherd the last group towards the exit, the oppressive heat smothering us.

The building groans, a death rattle that chills me more than any cold. The ceiling above us gives way, showering embers and debris. I shove the girls forward, pushing them towards Liam's waiting arms. A fiery brand lashes across my back, and I stagger, gritting my teeth against the agony.

"Kieran!" Finn's voice is distant, strained with fear and exertion. I can't see him through the smoke, but I feel his hand clamp onto my arm, dragging me away from the collapsing inferno.

We stumble out into the cool night, a world away from the hell inside. My back is a landscape of pain, every movement a fresh wave of torment. I watch as Liam and Finn usher the last of the girls to safety, their faces grim with the knowledge that not everyone made it out.

"Count?" I manage to ask, my voice hoarse.

"Most," Finn answers, his face shadowed. "Not all."

Guilt and relief wage war within me, a bitter cocktail that threatens to bring me to my knees. But I stand, bearing the weight of both the living and the lost, the burns on my back a testament to the night we fought fire and fate to save those we could.

Sloane's silhouette emerges like a wraith from the smoke, her form barely distinguishable against the backdrop of chaos. The rifle is slung over her shoulder, a stark reminder of the role she played tonight.

"Hey, it's alright now," her voice cuts through the lingering terror, soothing the women huddled together on the frigid concrete. "You're safe."

Her words are a balm, and I watch as tear-streaked faces lift towards her, their eyes reflecting a tumult of fear and gratitude. Sloane moves among them, her touch gentle, her presence a pillar of strength amidst the rubble of their shattered world.

"Kieran." Finn's voice is a low growl behind me, vibrating with barely suppressed fury. "Why the hell was Sloane here?"

Liam steps in, a buffer between Finn's wrath and my scorched skin. "She saved your ass more than once tonight. You'd do well to remember that."

"Because I can handle myself, Finnegan." Sloane's interruption is sharp, slicing through the tension. Her green eyes flash, emerald fire in the night. "And I've got your back, whether you like it or not."

"Dammit, Sloane, that's not the point!" Finn clenches his fists, the muscles in his jaw working furiously.

"Actually, it is." Sloane stands her ground, defiant. "I'm not some porcelain doll you need to lock away. I protected you tonight. You think those men would have hesitated to shoot you if I hadn't been there shooting them first?"

Finn's anger ebbs as he looks at his sister, his eyes taking in the smudges of soot on her face, the resolute set of her shoulders. The air crackles with the unspoken understanding that she is no longer the little girl he once shielded from the world.

"Fine," he grunts, the fight draining from him. "Just... be careful, okay?"

"Always am," Sloane replies with a smirk, her bravado untamed even by the night's horrors.

As I watch them, an odd sense of pride swells within me. Maybe it's the pain from my burns, or maybe it's the adrenaline still coursing through my veins, but something about this moment feels significant—a turning point in our tangled lives.

We are warriors in our own right, each of us scarred, each of us fighting demons both within and without. But together, we stand unbroken, ready to face whatever darkness comes next.

Chapter 17

Avalina

Sunlight filters through the canopy above in golden beams, dappling my skin as I wait in the secluded glen. A warm breeze rustles the leaves, carrying the earthy scent of pine and moss.

My heart skips a beat as Kieran emerges from the trees, his gaze piercing. "You're late," I say, a teasing lilt to my voice.

"My apologies." Kieran prowls toward me with a predatory grace, his eyes gleaming. "I had some business to attend to."

A shiver runs down my spine at his words, and I can't help but glance at his hands. Kieran and I had been seeing each other for a couple of weeks now, and I knew what *business* might mean. Or might not. I never knew and wasn't sure if I should ask.

I watch as Kieran shrugs out of his jacket, revealing lean, muscular arms wrapped with tattoos I now knew represented what mattered most to him. I had slowly been uncovering the meaning behind some of the ink I could see decorating his frame.

"Did you miss me?" Kieran asks softly.

I lift my chin, refusing to give in so easily. "Perhaps. If you're lucky."

A low chuckle rumbles in Kieran's chest. "Luck has nothing to do with it." He reaches out, tangling his fingers in my hair and tugging me closer. "Admit it. You want me as desperately as I want you."

His touch ignites a blaze beneath my skin. I could no more resist him than I could stop the sun from rising. "Yes," I breathe, my lips a hairsbreadth from his.

Triumph flashes in Kieran's eyes an instant before he claims my mouth in a searing kiss. I melt against him, twining my arms around his neck to pull him closer. His whiskey and smoke scent is intoxicating, as addictive as the most potent drug.

When Kieran finally lifts his head, I'm breathless, my senses reeling. "Do you see now why I can't stay away from you?" he rasps.

I smile up at him, my heart overflowing with tenderness and desire. "Just as you can't escape me. Not now that I know the truth."

Kieran's expression softens, his gaze searching. Brushing a stray lock of hair from my cheek, his touch turns achingly tender. "Nor would I want to."

My breath catches at his words. In that moment, I know with perfect clarity that Kieran speaks the truth.

The sun dips lower in the sky, its golden light filtering through the trees as Kieran and I make our way back down the wooded trail. A comfortable silence stretched between us, no words needed to express the peace and contentment we found in each other's presence.

Breathing deep, I inhaled the pine-scented air, my senses awakening to the surrounding beauty. Wildflowers dotted the rugged slope with bursts of color amid the greenery and birds chirped from the branches overhead.

I smile up at Kieran, warmth flooding through me at his presence in one of my favorite places. At this moment, I want nothing more than to freeze time, to remain here with him, cocooned in nature's embrace.

My foot snags on a rebellious root jutting out from the ground, and I stumble forward. Kieran's reflexes are swift, a testament to the predator lurking beneath his human veneer, but even he can't prevent my hand from scraping against the rugged bark of an oak tree. Pain lances through my palm, a bright red bloom of blood welling up.

"Damn," I hiss, more at my clumsiness than the sting of the wound.

"Let me see." Kieran's voice is a low purr, threaded with concern and something darker. Before I can protest, he takes my injured hand in his, inspecting it with an intensity that sends a shiver down my spine. Then, his tongue darts out, lapping at the crimson bead with a deliberate slowness that is both shocking and undeniably erotic.

"Kieran!" My breath catches, a mingled gasp of surprise and awakening hunger.

"Better?" He looks up, eyes gleaming with a feral light that matches the hint of blood on his lips.

"Y-yes," I stammer, my body aflame with a heat that has nothing to do with my minor injury.

He steps closer, and I'm suddenly aware of the solidity of his body, the barely restrained power that hums beneath his skin. With a grace that belies his size, Kieran backs me into the rough embrace of the tree behind me. His mouth descends upon mine, demanding and insistent. This kiss is a claiming, a fierce melding of lips and teeth that speaks of a hunger too long denied.

Kieran's hand envelopes mine, deftly guiding them upwards until they rest against the tree's rough and biting bark. My body instinctively reacts, arching itself into Kieran's as I feel the swell of his hard length pressing against my aching core. A moan escapes my lips as I'm engulfed in a wave of desire, but Kieran is already there, swallowing the sounds as if they were the sweetest nectar.

His hand moves to cradle my jaw, thumb caressing the sensitive skin there before trailing up to wrap around my throat—a gentle pressure, a silent reminder of the danger and thrill that he embodies. I move my arm, hands seeking the strength of his back, needing to pull him impossibly closer.

But as my fingers brush over his shirt, he hisses—a sound of pain so raw it sears through the haze of my desire. I freeze, the reality of the moment crashing back.

"Kieran? What's wrong?"

He tries to capture my gaze again, to pull me back into the spell we were weaving together, but I've seen—felt—something he can't hide. My heart races, not just with passion now, but with a dawning concern for this enigmatic man who has become my anchor in a world I no longer fully understand.

"Show me," I demand, my voice firm despite the tremor that runs through me.

"Nothing to worry about," he grumbles, the lines of his face tightening in a way that tells me he's lying.

But Kieran Calder doesn't give in easily, and I know that whatever he's concealing, it's serious. I may have lost memories of our past, but I trust the bond that thrums between us, a connection that defies logic and reason—a connection that I'm not willing to let him break, not when it could mean losing him all over again.

His broad shoulders shift as he takes a step back, a shadow crossing his normally impassive face. The scent of pine and damp earth mingles with the iron tang of my blood, but it's the pained expression in Kieran's eyes that anchors me to the spot.

"Kieran, you're hurt," I say, my voice laced with worry. "Please, let me see."

For a moment, he hesitates, a silent battle raging behind his stormy gaze. Then, with a resigned sigh, he slowly peels off his shirt, revealing his back to me. My breath catches at the sight. Angry burns mar his skin, some areas blistered and red, others an ominous, deeper shade. It looks like he's been clawed by fire itself.

"God, Kieran, what happened?" The question is a whisper, my fingertips itching to touch, to heal, yet afraid of causing more pain.

He doesn't meet my eyes as he speaks, his voice low and strained. "Sean O'Neil has... he took women, trapped them like animals and set fire to the place." His jaw clenches. "I couldn't stand by, Avalina. I had to get them out."

The scene unfolds in my mind, nightmarish and brutal. Kieran, stepping into the flames of hell to be the savior for those who had no one else. My heart swells with a fierce pride mixed with a terrifying realization of how close I could be to losing him.

"Kieran, you could have died," I murmur, my hands hovering over the scorched canvas of his skin, the heat radiating onto my palms.

"Perhaps," he admits, finally looking at me, his eyes dark pools of intensity. "But there are things worth risking everything for."

"Like saving innocents from a monster," I assert, trying to ignore the way my voice breaks.

"Like saving innocents," he echoes, a twisted smile touching his lips. "But make no mistake, Lina, I am a monster too. I've just chosen to live by a code."

The declaration sends shivers down my spine, not out of fear, but from the raw honesty that bleeds from his words. He stands before me, a man carved from darkness and light, his actions both terrifying and achingly beautiful.

"Your code makes you different," I argue, reaching out to trace the lines of his burns gently. "It makes you better than him."

"Does it?" Kieran's voice is barely audible, his hand coming up to cover mine, pressing it against the warmth of his injury. "Or does it simply make me a monster of a different kind?"

In his touch, I feel the weight of his sins and the strength of his resolve. "Your code is why I'm here with you now," I confess as I lean forward, pressing a soft kiss to the edge of one of his burns. "It's why I can't walk away, why I don't want to walk away. I want to remember."

"Whether you remember or not, I'll be here as long as you want me," Kieran vows, his voice rumbling through the stillness of the forest, wrapping around us like a promise.

Chapter 18

Avalina

Shelving books at the library is one of my favorite things. Getting to see the books and putting them back in their places, the spines a kaleidoscope of color against the dark wood.

A light green book with accents of gold calls to me from the shelf above the one I'm working at, and I reach up to tug it down so I can inspect the tome. It's old, covered in book cloth instead of a printed cover. Opening it, I realize it contains ancient tales and myths. Flipping through the pages, my gaze snags on an illustration of swans taking flight.

I am so lost in thought I don't hear the footsteps behind me crossing the floor. Not until a deep, gravelly voice speaks behind me.

"What are you reading?"

I jump in surprise, my hands fumbling as I almost drop the book. I whirl around to find Kieran leaning against the wall, watching me with an unreadable expression.

"Kieran! You startled me!" I exclaim, pressing a hand to my chest. My heart was pounding, though not entirely from shock.

"Sorry, it looks like that book must be good," he says, pushing away from the wall. "I came to see you. To see if you wanted to go to dinner."

I grin and fight the urge to fidget, my nerves getting the better of me as I toy with my necklace. The one I now know is from Kieran.

"You could have called. Or texted." I bite my lip.

Kieran eyed the movement. "I know. But I wanted to see you. Plus, I've always wanted to make out with a naughty librarian."

I laugh at this and playfully shove at him. "That's not happening, buddy."

His smirk tells me he thinks differently.

I gesture to the cart of books I'm in the middle of shelving. "I'm busy right now. But I could have dinner with you."

"What time do you want me to pick you up?"

"7?" I ask, thinking I'd need time to get home and feed Conan and change out of my work clothes.

"7 it is then," he replies, reaching across the cart to grasp me around the waist and tug me to him, capturing my lips in a kiss that had me questioning my no make out in the library rules.

He pulls away and tucks a stray hair behind my ear. "I'll see you at 7," he says before turning and walking away.

My mind is reeling, caught up in the surge of emotions racing through me, when a laugh interrupts my thoughts.

"So *that's* what has been keeping you distracted lately."

I turn to see Mavis standing at the end of the bookcase, a hand resting on her growing baby bump. She is due in a couple of weeks with her first child and although Sarah and I have both told her to stay off her feet and rest as much as she can at the reference desk, Mavis has been doing as she pleases.

The telltale heat of a blooming blush creeps up my neck, and I suddenly find the books in my hand *very* interesting. "I have no idea what you're referring to, Mavis." I try, but fail, to hide my smile.

Mavis steps closer to me. "I need all the details. You've been holding out on me! I mean, Kieran Calder!" she whispers this last part.

"I know, I know! I haven't told anyone, even Iris. Mainly because Iris seemed to think he wasn't good enough for me." I frown.

Mavis glares. "Screw that. I want all the details."

I laugh. "Okay, but not... here."

Mavis nods. "What about this weekend? You can come over to my place and help me finish up the nursery while you tell me all the steamy details."

"Okay, sounds good."

Later that evening, I'm standing at my closet door, wondering what to wear. Kieran and I have seen each other a few times now, but it is always at his place or mine. By him seeking me out at the library today, plus going to dinner together tonight, we are moving away from feeling like we have to hide our relationship in the shadows.

Conan brushes up against my leg and meows, looking up at me with pleading eyes. "You want me to pick you up, bud?" Reaching down, I put my not so small tabby cat in my arms, while he curls up and nestles close, kneading in the fabric of my soft, fluffy robe.

"What do you think I should wear tonight, hmm?" I walk over to a simple black dress, pulling it out to take a better look. Conan yawns, and I chuckle. "Yeah, I think you're right. It's too simple."

Next, I finger a long, gauzy violet dress, which might be more suited to warmer, spring weather instead of the chilly autumn nights, but I think it would pair well with a pair of ankle boots and a fitted faux leather jacket. Conan swipes at the fabric, trying to play with it. I laugh. "Purple it is, then."

It isn't long after that I touch up my makeup and sweep my copper hair up into a simple, slightly messy bun when a knock sounds at the door. Answering it, I can't help the swell of gratitude for Conan's choice of clothing when I spot Kieran wearing dark dress pants and a navy sweater pulled over a white button-up shirt.

"One second, I just need to feed Conan, so he doesn't tear us my curtains or devour my pillow while I'm gone." I say to Kieran as I step back to let him into my apartment.

His lips twitch. "Has he done that before?" Kieran asks as he shuts the door behind him.

"No," I reply over my shoulder, grabbing the cat food down from the cabinet. "Well, not exactly. It's a long story."

"Good thing we have all night, then." I glance up through my lashes at Kieran from where I'm kneeling, putting Conan's food bowl on the floor.

"That's rather presumptuous of you." I respond haughtily, trying my best to mask the heat flowing through my veins at the look he's giving me as I kneel in front of him.

The moment stretches between us, and I can't think of a single thing to say to break the rising tension.

Kieran reaches his hand out to help me up, and I take it, silently rising to my feet in front of him.

"What are you thinking about?" he asks as he tilts his head. I feel like his eyes can see right through my facade, to the nerves that are racing through my veins.

I wring my hands together and look down, embarrassment heating my neck. "Sometimes I have dreams. But I'm not sure if they are dreams or memories."

"What do you dream about?" he asks, eyes narrowing.

"You. Me. Us. We're having sex." I stammer, not needing a mirror to know red is blooming across my chest and face.

I glance up to see Kieran's hands fisted by his sides. My mouth opens and closes, but no words come out and I wish the ground would just open me up and swallow me whole.

"We should talk."

"Talk?"

"Yes," Kieran drawls. "Talk." He runs a hand through his hair, disheveling it in the best way possible, and I try hard to not bite my lip. Kieran places his hands on the nearby kitchen counter, his face suddenly serious. "From our conversations before, I was the only one you had this conversation with, but it may have changed."

I move to slide onto the barstool across the counter from him, waiting for him to continue.

"With sex, I like to be in control." He pauses and examines my face at this, looking for any sign that I'm about to run. I'm not. While he's right that I don't recall having this conversation with anyone else, much less him, most of my romance books on my e-reader have elements of BDSM, so I'm not completely ignorant.

I am, however, shocked that we're having this conversation and again have to remind myself that Kieran remembers our relationship, and that I'm the one who this is all new for. Well, new again.

Knowing we've been here before gives me a confidence I didn't know I had, so I ask, "What else do you like?"

Kieran's eyes darken at that, the brown deepening to the color of the forest at night.

Leaning forward, he pulls the invisible string between us tight as he answers. "Telling you when to come and making you do it over and over again until tears are streaming down your face as you scream my name in ecstasy. And then you kneeling at my feet, begging for more."

All the air escapes my lungs and heat travels directly to my center. It takes me a few tries before I can voice my next thought. "And what did I like?"

A smirk straight from the devil plays upon his lips and I realize I've shown my hand with my question. I don't think I have it in me to care if he knows what effect his words have on me.

"My hands wrapped around that pretty throat as your pussy wept for my cock."

I'm practically gasping for air now. "And did I have a safe word?"

Surprise flashes across Kieran's face. "You remember that?"

"No, but I've read about it."

"It was daffodil."

"Kieran," I breathe, the name rising from some place deep inside me.

And then Kieran moves faster than I can track, and his mouth descends on mine in a searing kiss that steals my breath away, binding me to him in a way that is impossible to escape. Not that I want to.

My lips part with a soft gasp and Kieran takes advantage, his tongue sweeping forward to meet mine, leaving the taste of whiskey behind.

I feel dizzy with desire, clinging to him as my knees threaten to cave under the weight of my passion.

Kieran wraps his arms around me, pulling me flush against him. The warmth of his body seeps into mine, and I slide my hands up his chest to wrap around his neck, deepening the kiss.

A low groan rumbles in Kieran's chest, vibrating against my lips and sending a jolt straight to my core. I want more—to drive him to the edge of control and beyond. To ignite the barely restrained passion I sense within him. Kieran is always so restrained and calculated. I want him undone.

Kieran's hands trail down to my hips before lifting me up. I arch into him with a soft moan, wrapping my legs around his body as he carries me to the couch in the living room, sitting me astride his lap.

Kieran moves from my lips to trail hot, open-mouthed kisses along my jaw and down the sensitive skin of my neck. I tip my head back with a sigh, desire pooling low in my belly.

"Tell me to stop," Kieran rasps against my collarbone. His hands slide under the neckline of my dress, calloused fingers igniting sparks along my skin. "Tell me you don't want this."

"I will never tell you that," I reply breathlessly, "but we're going to be late for dinner." I tangle my fingers in his hair and guide his mouth back to mine, kissing him with a hunger that matches his own.

"I've got all the dinner I need right here," Kieran growls low in his throat, the sound shuddering through me. His hands slide down to cup my breasts, teasing my nipples into tight peaks that strain against the violet fabric.

Heat floods my veins as I arch into his touch with a soft cry. Tugging at his sweater, Kieran breaks our kiss to yank it over his head and tosses it behind him. I'm desperate to feel his bare skin against mine and fumble with the buttons of his shirt, fingers clumsy with anticipation.

As I push the shirt from his shoulders, my fingers brush against the ridged scars that mar his chest and abdomen, but that isn't what catches my eye.

My gaze snags on a tattoo on Kieran's broad chest. It is an exact match to the necklace I wear, the curved lines intertwining just about his heart. My hand automatically lifts, tracing the edges of the ink.

I understood in this moment that no matter what I couldn't remember of this man, of our time together, I was etched in his soul, more permanent than any scar.

"Now you know," Kieran interrupts my thoughts, his voice low.

"Know what?"

"I would have carried you with me forever, no matter which way the tides turned. If you remembered, or not. If we were together, or not. It wouldn't have mattered. You left your mark on me a long time ago, Lina."

At a loss for words, I lower my lips to the lines my fingers were tracing and kiss them.

My stomach drops as I am suddenly in the air, being carried down the hall towards my bedroom. Sitting me on the bed, Kieran kneels before me.

"May I?" he asks. I nod and he moves like honey, trailing his hands up my legs in an unhurried pace, slowly slipping my boots off.

Hooded eyes meet mine as his hands began a deliciously slow torment up the inside of my thighs, meandering in their exploration. But instead of going to my dripping core like I'm envisioning in my head, Kieran smirks as he grabs the hem of my dress to lift it over my head.

I couldn't stop the frustrated growl that left my lips.

Kieran just continues to his sly fox grin as he reaches around to unclasp my bra and then his hands are traveling to my hips again, gripping my underwear and oh so slowly pulling them down my heated flesh.

"Didn't anyone ever tell you that patience is a virtue?"

"Fuck you," I hiss.

"Oh, you will, don't worry." he grins.

He pulls back enough to strip off his pants and then he's on me, pushing me down against the bed and folding his body over mine. His lips crash into mine as his body weighs me down, the sudden contact too much and not enough.

I thread my fingers in his hair as I pant between kisses, shifting my hips in an attempt to ease the ache that's building between my thighs.

"I want to hear you say it, Lina."

I pout and nip at Kieran's neck in irritation, wanting to leave a mark on him, the same way I know he's marked my soul.

A dark chuckle tickles my ear before Kieran leans back to look me in the eye. "Use your words, Lina."

I blow a breath between my teeth before answering. "I want you to fuck me, Kieran."

Thankfully, Kieran doesn't tease me further, and instead trails kisses down my neck and shoulder, a constellation that only he knows.

"Please," I gasp. I lift my hips up, angling towards him. Kieran pushes inside in one slow glide, forcing a shudder out of my body and breath out of my lungs. We both still for just a moment, all too aware of how well we fit together, and then we're moving once again.

Here, my forgotten memories are abandoned, discarded like paper on the wind. All that matters is the blood rushing in my veins, singing to the man currently seated inside of me. It's sex, but it's more than sex. It's coming home, and I'm unsure which one of us is finding ourselves again, me or Kieran.

I wrap myself around Kieran, holding on as he grips my hips and fucks me slow, trailing kisses over my neck and breasts, teasing my nipples into firm points that have me arching against him. Slowly the pressure builds and Kieran's hand moves between us, brushing and circling my clit with languid strokes. He's in no rush to wring out every drop of pleasure he can from my body.

I'm caught in a web that I'm desperate to escape but never want to leave. The pleasure is intense, clouding over all of my senses until nothing is left but the sensation of Kieran's body on mine. My past that I can't remember, the accident, everything else melts away.

Another brush of his lips under my ear, a swipe of his fingers at my core, and I'm crying out, muscles tensing in pleasure so sweet it feels like I'll drown. Kieran grunts and then he's moving with me, chasing his own release.

We fall back to the bed with me curled on top of Kieran, my head resting on his chest, again tracing my fingers on the dark lines there.

"What does it mean?" I ask.

"It's a Celtic knot called Serch Bythol, which means everlasting love in Welsh."

"And when did you get the tattoo?" I gaze up at him to see his hooded eyes locked onto mine, their depths unreadable.

"The night I gave you the necklace."

I settled back onto his chest, pondering his words, one hand on my necklace and the other on Kieran's chest.

It wasn't long until sleep settled over me like a soft blanket, and for the first time in months, I simply dreamed.

I awake to the rich scent of coffee, and my mouth waters at the thought of sugary caffeine on my tongue. I stretch languidly, my body pleasantly sore as memories of the night before flash through my mind—Kieran's hands and mouth exploring every inch of my body, his whispered promises and fervent pleas ringing in my ears.

"I dreamed of you, even when you didn't dream of me. It's always been you, Avalina. Always you."

The creak of a door made me turn. Kieran emerges in the doorway, dressed once more in dark jeans and a black shirt. His hair is mussed from sleep, his gaze intense as it settles on me.

"I brought you coffee," he says, holding out a steaming mug.

Sitting up with the sheet around me, I reach out for the cup of divine nectar. "Trying to get on my good side?"

Kieran's mouth quirks. "Too late for that now, Lina." His gaze dipped to the exposed skin at my neck, darkening. "I already got everything I wanted from you last night."

Heat floods my cheeks as I bring the mug to my lips. The coffee was hot and sweet, just the way I liked it. "How did you know?" I wonder aloud.

Kieran sits down beside me, his arm brushing against mine. "I've always known you, Lina. Even when you don't know yourself."

I stare at him, questions rising in my throat. I think of the familiar way he touched me, the secrets we had shared in the dark. Even though I can't remember our time together from before the accident, it feels right, being here with Kieran. The only thing missing was my acceptance of this bond that tugged tight between us.

Sipping my coffee, a flash of insight dawns. Somewhere along the way, the memories I was missing in my relationship with Kieran began to feel less like an unbreachable mist. Curiosity burns the mental fog away, revealing the path that had been before me all along, waiting for me.

Chapter 19

Avalina

The warmth of an autumn sun that refuses to acknowledge the seasonal decree caresses my skin like a lover's lingering touch. I'm lounging on a bench in Kingsale park, the varnished wood slightly cool beneath me, as I savor the final drops of summer's kiss. Lethargic bees hum drowsily around the audaciously blooming roses that have stubbornly pushed their way through the quilt of amber leaves carpeting the earth.

I sip my iced tea, its crispness a stark contrast to the mellow day, and let my gaze drift from the pages of the book cradled in my lap. The words dance and blend into the scenery, a tale of passion and heartache that resonates with something deep within me, something lost to the shadows of amnesia.

"Hey, Avalina!" The voice prickles at the edges of my solitude, jarring me back to reality.

Amanda and Claire come bounding towards me, their runners' high casting a glow on their faces. Sweat beads on their foreheads like tiny diamonds under the soft light filtering through the trees.

"Didn't expect to find you here," Amanda pants, brushing a strand of hair from her eyes while Claire slows down beside her, both catching their breath.

"Seems like the perfect day to get lost in a book," I reply, marking my page with a finger and setting the book aside. My voice feels out of place in the serenity of the park, like a ripple disturbing still waters.

"Are you enjoying the weather?" Claire asks, bending over to stretch her calves, her movements graceful despite the exertion.

"Absolutely," I say, watching a fallen leaf pirouette slowly to the ground. "It's as if nature itself is confused, caught between seasons." It mirrors my own inner turmoil, the old and new warring within me for dominance.

"Looks pretty decided to me," Amanda says with a grin. "Summer's having one last fling before giving up the ghost."

We laugh, and for a moment, everything feels almost normal—almost as if the accident that stole my memories never happened. But it did, and I can't forget that, even if I've forgotten so much else.

Amanda's laughter fades, and she shifts her weight from one foot to the other, a familiar glint of determination in her eyes. "You should come out with us tonight," she insists, the invitation less an offer and more a command.

"Thanks, but I'll pass," I murmur, the scent of damp earth and decaying leaves mingling with the tang of my iced tea. The park's tranquility is a stark contrast to the tension that starts to coil within me.

"Come on, Avalina. It's been ages since you joined us. It'll be like old times," Amanda presses, her tone brooking no argument.

I stand up, brushing bits of grass off my jeans. A fluttering in my chest tells me I need to stand firm. "Old times are just that—old. I'm not the same person I was before the accident."

"Exactly why you need this," she retorts, her voice rising slightly as if volume could sway me. "You're too wrapped up in this...this solitude."

My patience frays like the edges of the book in my hands. "No, Amanda. I'm finding peace. Something I couldn't when I was constantly bending to fit into everyone else's mold."

She huffs, planting her hands on her hips. "It's always been this way, Avalina. Why can't you just go along with it?"

"Because 'always' doesn't apply anymore." My words are sharp, a shard of glass glinting in the sunlight. "I'm done pleasing everyone at the cost of losing myself."

"Are you saying you don't need us?" Her question slices through the air, leaving a trail of bitter accusation.

"Maybe I'm saying we shouldn't be friends anymore if this is how it's going to be," I admit, the admission tasting like acid on my tongue. Even as I say it, I feel the finality of it, a chapter closing in the story of who I once was.

A leaf quivers as it tumbles down from an overhanging branch, landing silently onto the path where our shadows mingle in disarray. The tension between Amanda and me hangs heavy, a thick fog that refuses to lift, even as Claire steps in, her voice a soothing balm in the aftermath of our bitter exchange.

"Look, Amanda," she begins, her tone steady yet imploring, "Avalina's been through a lot. After the accident, after all those memories slipped away from her grasp, she's not... She's not who she used to be."

I watch Claire's careful gaze shift towards me, full of understanding, her eyes soft like dew clinging to the petals of the late-blooming roses.

"And that's okay," Claire continues, her words wrapping around us like a shawl against the chill of conflict. "We should be here for her, supporting her journey to rediscover herself, not forcing her into the mold of who she was before."

Claire's plea hangs between us, and I can feel the sincerity of her intentions radiating like the warmth of the sun. Her hand finds mine, squeezing gently, grounding me.

"Can't you see?" Claire says, turning back to Amanda, "She doesn't need to fit into our expectations. She needs to find out who she is on her own terms."

The pressure in my chest loosens slightly, but the embers of defiance still smolder within. I lift my chin, feeling the resolve harden around my heart like armor forged from newfound self-assurance.

"Amanda," I interject, my voice unwavering, "you're trying to stuff me back into a box—a box splintered by the crash, one where the corners no longer align with who I am now."

My fingers brush against the rough bark of a nearby oak, its gnarled surface mirroring the complexity of my thoughts.

"I don't desire the life I had before," I assert, the taste of truth rich on my tongue. "I yearn to explore this new existence—messy, uncharted, and raw. Maybe it terrifies you because you want the old Avalina, the one who danced to your whims. But she's gone, dissolved like mist at dawn."

The air shifts, carrying with it the scent of damp earth and the undercurrent of change. I stand firm, the remnants of my past scattering with the fallen leaves around us, making room for the blossoms of who I'm becoming.

The silence stretches between us, a chasm filled with the weight of words unsaid. Amanda's breath hitches, a soft sound almost lost to the rustling leaves around us. Her gaze flickers to mine, hesitant and searching, as if she's looking for the Avalina she once knew in the depths of my green eyes.

"Look, Avalina..." she begins, her voice lower, the sharp edge of earlier confrontations softened into something more pliable—regret, perhaps. "I—I'm sorry."

The words hang there, simple, yet charged with the potential for change. I watch, motionless, as Amanda struggles to find her footing on this new ground we've stumbled upon, her usual confidence wavering like a flame in the autumn breeze.

"Sorry for what?" My question isn't meant to be cruel, but it is necessary. I need to understand—to hear her acknowledge the shift in our tenuous bond.

"For trying to force you back into... into who you were before," she admits, and her voice cracks ever so slightly, revealing the vulnerability she often keeps shielded behind bravado. "It's just hard, you know? To see you change and not know where I fit into your life anymore."

A pang of empathy surges within me, warming the chill that had settled around my heart. I realize then that change doesn't only alter the person it happens to; its ripples touch everyone in their orbit.

"You don't have to fit into my life, Amanda," I respond, choosing my words with care, desiring reconciliation over resentment. "We can find a new way to be friends—if that's what you want."

"I do, Avalina, I really do." The sincerity in her eyes is the balm to the scrapes left by our quarrel. "I just miss you, that's all."

"Then let's start anew," I offer, extending my hand towards her. It's an invitation, a truce, a bridge over the troubled waters of our past disagreements.

Her fingers entwine with mine, warm and firm, and something inside me unfurls—a hope that maybe, just maybe, we can navigate this complex journey of rediscovery together.

Chapter 20

KIERAN

Glancing at the clock, I step into the shower, feeling the warm water cascade over my skin. I had promised Avalina dinner tonight, and while she wouldn't mind if it wasn't ready when she arrived, I wanted everything to be perfect for her. As the steam enveloped me, I let go of the tension that had been building up throughout the day.

Sean is up to no good, I know it. As far as Finn can tell, Sean has no idea that we were behind freeing the people we found in the warehouse that night, and now he is on high alert, trying to smoke out whoever betrayed him. As long as Finn and Slone have intel that keeps us a step ahead of Sean, we should be good, but I still won't feel easy until he's longer an issue.

Grabbing a towel as I step out of the shower, I dry off my damp skin as I walk to my closet. Taking a quick look at my options, I choose a pair of dark jeans and a navy sweater, trying to hop into the jeans as I walk down the hall.

Once I step into the kitchen, muscle memory takes over as I effortlessly set the pot of water to boil and deftly slice the garlic and onions. I cut quickly, the feel of flesh giving way under my blade a familiar comfort.

The rush to this point has me feeling scattered, my focus torn as my own demon scratches under my skin, craving something to gnaw on. I can't help but wonder if this restlessness has something to do with Lina. She crawled under my skin and made herself at home, right next to my monster.

The sauce is simmering when a knock on my door sounds.

I open my door to find Avalina in a slinky red dress that molds to her curves and leaves nothing to the imagination. Not that I need to imagine any inch of her at this part. I've got her mapped like a constellation across my heart.

I arch an eyebrow her way. "We're staying in, remember?"

"I know. I just thought I'd wear something different for a change. I'm always in jeans at the library."

She walks towards my kitchen, and I don't try to hide the smile slowly bleeding across my face. Lina thinks she is being clever, but with the mood I'm in, she's going to get more than she bargained for.

Sometimes Lina forgets what I am, a monster that doesn't mind playing with their food first.

She wants to play? Fine. I'll even let her think she's winning, at least for now.

I watch her saunter towards the sauce bubbling on the stove, and she dips a wooden spoon in the mixture as red as her dress before bringing it to her lips to taste. I'm impressed at my ability to keep my face a neutral mask as she moans at the taste.

My hands itch to give her something else to taste, but I clear my throat and adjust my pants before walking behind her to grab the spoon, lifting it to my own lips to taste as I press my hardness against the swell of her ass.

I don't miss the way she bites her bottom lip.

"Hmm, needs more salt."

I cage Lina in my arms as I reach to the counter for the salt before slowly stirring the sauce and turning off the burner.

Trailing a hand down her arm, I kiss the spot under her ear. "It's ready. Go sit down and I'll bring it to you."

She looks up at me, suspicion flashing in her eyes at my tone, but moves to do as I ask.

I almost regret the command, as once she sits down, the red silk rides even higher up her creamy thighs.

I've interrogated countless people, slowly tortured them until they gave me the answers I sought. I've honed my mind and body into lethal precision because my life demanded it of me.

But all of that threatens to unravel as I eye Lina from the kitchen, plating her dinner while my inner demon roars to break free and devour her instead.

Placing dinner on the table, I'm mindful to keep my carefully cultivated smirk on my face, lounging back in the chair like I'm in no rush.

I've done this before, this waiting game. But normally I'm also not being tortured by it.

"How was work?" I ask.

"It was good. We have a few more authors on the schedule for book tour stops and we're going to coordinate with the local bookstore for some midnight release parties."

"Sounds like your plan to get more buzz and patrons is working. Sarah must be excited."

"She is. She even finally agreed to let me take over the social media accounts, which I think will help reach a whole new audience."

"I'm really proud of you, Lina."

She dips her head down, tucking a loose strand of hair behind her ear before toying with her necklace. *My* necklace. The one I gave her.

Fidgeting, she glances up at me through her lashes. "Thank you, Kieran."

I've seen this woman lead an entire classroom of children through the library with ease, but she still gets nervous when I compliment her. I'll just have to do it more.

Reaching across the table, I lightly brush my hand across hers, watching the shiver that she can't suppress.

My entire life I've sought more thieves and criminals to punish, eager to let my beast out of its cage.

It wasn't until I met Avalina that I realized I could find release in her, in the pleasure of her body but also in the comfort of her presence. She calms my beast, tames it into a slumbering dragon I know would torch anything that dared to threaten her.

Moving through the rest of dinner is a test of patience, as the thread of desire is taut between us, undeniable in every line of Lina's body.

I push my chair away from the table, grabbing our plates. "Ready for dessert?" I ask.

"What kind of dessert?" Lina purrs and leans forward.

"Ice cream," I deadpan as I pile the dishes and walk to the kitchen.

I glance back to quickly turn away again, unable to hide my smile at the look of disappointment on Avalina's face.

"I was hoping for something different."

"Different from ice cream? What did you have in mind?" I turn to see Lina glaring at me, and I can't hide the chuckle that worms its way past my oblivious façade.

Stalking towards her, I brace my arms against the back of her chair, leaning in to inhale her jasmine and sandalwood scent, the intoxicating fragrance going straight to my cock now straining against my pants.

Slowly, I reach down and trail the edge of my fingers along her silk dress, grazing her skin as I pull the fabric higher up her thighs.

"Hmmm," I hum along her neck, my nose tracing her throbbing pulse, "someone is suddenly very quiet."

Brushing the insight of her quivering legs, I stay away from her core, which is no doubt dripping all over my mahogany dining chair at this point. I make a mental note to never clean this chair again.

Avalina writhes under me, eager for me to continue. I chuckle, knowing that drawing out her desire heightens it even more.

"Kieran, please," Avalina moans, "stop teasing me."

Leaning over her, I move my hand up to grip her jaw, slowly licking my way up the path I just trailed with my breath. "But teasing makes you scream my name as you come all over my cock."

The cutest growl reverberates behind Lina's gritted teeth, but it is swept away in a gasp as I grab the hem of her dress and pull it over her head, tossing it to the side.

The sight of Lina in that red dress was torture, but seeing her naked, realizing that she wasn't wearing a stitch of fabric under that silk, has me crashing into insanity and not giving a fuck.

I tuck my arms under her and pick her up, carrying her to my bedroom, ideas flashing through my mind of just how I can pay her back for this delicious, mind-numbing torment.

Arms curl around me tightly as I set Lina down on my black sheets, her copper hair spread out under her. She tugs my head down for a kiss and I take advantage of her distraction, pulling a silk tie out from hiding and wrapping it around her wrists.

Half-lidded eyes meet mine as she tugs on the silk binding her arms above her head.

I dip my head lower, swirling my tongue around a taut nipple. "All you have to say is your safe word, and I stop." I looked up at her. "Do you want to stop?"

Her eyes flash open, wide and alarmed before narrowing. "Don't you dare fucking stop."

"That's what I thought. But don't take that tone with me, brat. You got yourself into this."

Kissing her other breast, I rise to release my cock from my pants, shucking them and my shirt off faster than I thought possible.

I force myself to resume my lazy torment and drag my way down her body, ignoring the primal need to sheath myself to the hilt in her welcoming heat. Returning to her drenched pussy that I had been teasing moments before, I dip one finger inside of her with teasing strokes.

Nipping at the inside of Lina's thigh, I slap her pretty pink folds when she tries to arch towards me in an attempt to press herself to my mouth.

"Stay still." The command was all sharp edges, but that knife point had all of Avalina's soft curves flushing crimson.

"You've made such a mess of yourself." I lightly trace the outside of her pussy. "Someone has to clean this up,". I chided, keeping that hard line to my voice instead of the desperation I felt to dive into her soaking core.

Grabbing her thighs, I push down, holding her in place. My tongue darts out, licking up her juices and savoring her taste, before I move up to her clit, lazily drawing circles around her nub before bringing it into my mouth and sucking. Lina does her best to keep her body still, but I can feel her muscles trembling under my hands.

Humming with her clit between my teeth earns me a breathy gasp from above my head. Looking up, I see tears creeping from the corners of her eyes and down the sides of her face.

Moving over her but keeping our bodies separate, I lick away each of those salt encrusted orbs. I can't help the shudder that comes over me. "I love it when you trust me enough to make you cry." I press my body down, my throbbing cock pressing against her weeping core.

I untie her arms and nails immediately prick my flesh as Lina wraps her arms around me, trying to tug my cock closer to her demanding heat as she arches up to me.

My hand shoots out and cages Avalina's throat. "I thought I told you to stay still." She whines as I draw back and slap her pussy.

Bending down to press a kiss on her lips, my other hand squeezes her hip as I nip along her jaw and neck, where the necklace I gave her gleams in the fading light of day.

Pressing my cock at her entrance, we both groan. "Be a good girl," I hiss, "and show me how much you want my come."

Lina whines at my command but keeps her body still as I gradually inch inside of her, knowing I'm not going to last much longer. Even now, I can feel my body getting tight and my monster roaring to thrust into her so hard I leave bruises.

Shaking off the urge to punish, I focus on my pace, driving into her a little harder, a little faster, each time our bodies meet, Lina's whines turning into animalistic moans that my throat is echoing, my climax so close I can taste it.

Avalina's muscles clench around me, her nails digging into my back, and she arches and writhes, unable to control her limbs any longer. The pinprick of pain sends me tumbling over the edge after her, and I fall into the sweet release of darkness.

Chapter 21

Avalina

The scent of olive oil and warm bread engulf my senses as I take another huge bite of bread, the tang of rosemary blooming on my tongue. Bella Luna is one of my favorite places to eat, and it's not just because of the fresh bread, so warm steam escapes the loaf as I tear it apart. The atmosphere is cozy and friendly, with warm lighting and deep seats you can relax in.

Amanda and Claire sit across from me, chatting about work projects, while Iris sits next to me, scanning the restaurant menu like it holds a secret only she can decode.

We're all meeting up for the first time since the Preston Gala a few weeks ago, since we've all been busy with different work projects, many of which were kicked off at the gala, a place more for making connections than truly having fun.

Sarah and I have been busy at the library now that Mavis is taking some time before her baby arrives. I've taken it upon myself to make Kingsdale a sought-out spot for authors on book tours and I've reached out to local writers to get the ball rolling.

I'm busy munching on some bread and thinking about the authors I should reach out to next when Amanda says a name that catches my attention.

"I'm so glad we're finally getting to catch up, but I can't stay out late tonight. I've got a big meeting in the morning with Kieran Calder."

"Kieran Calder?" Iris asks. "Why are you meeting with him?"

"His family owns an extensive amount of artwork, and the gallery is setting up a showing and they want to really expand the guest list. I think he's looking into selling some of the collection."

"Oh, what kind of art does he have?" Claire asks, then looks at me. "Avie, have you seen any of it?"

Amanda frowns. "Why would Avie have seen any of the Calder collection?"

I can feel Iris staring at me, her glare practically burning holes in the side of my head.

Taking a sip of water to clear the once delicious bread now feels like a lead weight at the bottom of my stomach, I clear my throat. "Kieran and I have been seeing each other."

"What?" Amanda practically screeches. "Since when?"

"Technically, since before my accident. But then with the accident, I forgot I was in a relationship with him. We've recently reconnected."

"And you knew?" Amanda turns and slaps Claire on the shoulder.

"Hey!" Claire holds up her hands in innocence. "Iris knew, too!"

"Why am I the last one to know?" Amanda pouts.

I reach across the table to grab Amanda's hands, trying to snuff out her anger with the desperate plea of my voice. "Because it's new. Well, new to me. It's awkward having Kieran remember me so well but I still feel like I'm discovering who Kieran is. I guess I wanted to protect that. Those of you at this table are the only ones who know."

Amanda huffs, but that she doesn't pull her hands away tells me she's at least a little mollified. "I guess I can understand that." Her gaze shifts, sharpens. "But you have to tell me everything now."

Groaning, I stuff another piece of bread in my mouth, wanting to avoid exactly what Amanda wants me to talk about.

Claire playfully shoves at Amanda. "Quit teasing Avie. You don't need all the details."

"Oh, come on, I just want to know if the rumors are true."

I pause eating, looking back and forth between my friends in confusion. "What rumors?"

Leaning across the table, Amanda whispers, "Is he good in bed? I've heard he rarely sleeps with a girl more than once and those that are lucky enough to be in his bed practically beg for the chance to go back."

My eyes widen and I have no chance to stop the crimson creeping up my cheeks in a flood.

Amanda's cackle fills the air.

It's Iris' birthday, and she decided all she wanted was a night out dancing. The shifting, colorful lights make our skin glow and our dresses shimmer as we sway and spin to the beat. The vibrating rumble of the music thrums through me as I move on the dance floor, surrounded by Claire, Iris, and Amanda. It's been a couple of weeks since I confessed my relationship to Kieran to all my friends, and I've been pleasantly surprised at how accepting they've been.

It's nice to be out with my friends in a place where conversation isn't the priority, where my fragmented memories can't bleed like ink stains that ruin everything they touch.

Surrounded by music, I can let everything go as my troubles are washed away with the rising crescendo. My friends and I may not agree on everything or have the same interests that we used to, but here I feel more connected to them than I have in a long time, without the pressure of trying to remember what was lost to the wreckage.

Our group dances on as the song gives way to another, with a deep bass pulse that pounds through me. As I twirl, I spot Amanda looking behind me, eyes widening as she gestures to the rest of the group. Leaning in, I can't hear her over the thumping tune, but I can understand the word her mouth is shaping. *Incoming.*

We tighten our circle, moving into defensive positions as a group of guys encroaches on our space. I see Iris snarl as someone comes up behind her to press against her, and she turns to give him a piece of her mind. I'm moving to help my sister when hands grip my hips and pull me backwards into a chest smelling of too much cologne and alcohol.

"Hands off," I bark to the person behind me, turning my head to see blue eyes and blonde curls resting above a drunken leer that is coming closer to my face.

"Oh, don't be like that baby," the creep says as he moves in to kiss me.

I grab the wrists anchored to my waist and dig in my nails before twisting and sending my elbow right into the jerk's gut.

"What the fuck?" the drunk mumbles.

I'm about to knee him in the groin when the scent of whiskey and sandalwood surrounds me, and I twist to see Kieran, looming like dark death incarnate in the shifting lights.

"She said hands off." Kieran's voice rumbles clearly through the space as bodies pause their movement to watch the drama unfold.

He turns to me, hand catching me under the chin to tilt my head up to his. "You okay, Lina?"

"Yeah, I'm fine. This guy has just had a little too much to drink." I smile brightly, trying to convince Kieran of what I'm saying.

Kieran's hooded glare says he thinks otherwise, but he'll play along. "You go with your friends," he says as he pushes me towards Claire. "We're going to go have a little chat." He grabs the drunk guy and practically drags him off the dance floor. No one tries to stop him. He's Kieran Calder. He probably owns this building.

I look over to Iris, who is staring wide eyes at the space Kieran just vacated. "Are you okay, Iris?"

Iris blinks as her gaze swivels to me. "Am I okay? What about you? That creep was all over you!"

I brush off her concern. "He was just drunk and stupid."

"No, Avie," Iris interrupts. "Drunk doesn't excuse being an asshole who wants to assault women. I hope Kieran rips him to shreds."

It's my turn to blink now, shocked at my sister agreeing with Kieran's actions.

"What, what do you think Kieran is doing with him?"

"Avie," Amanda laughs, "he's totally going to beat him up for touching you."

"What, no!" I look around for Kieran and the drunk. "There's no need for that."

Iris sweeps an arm around my shoulders and brings me close. "There is absolutely every need. I say so and it's my birthday. Just think of it as Kieran's birthday present to me!"

I can't help but laugh at the bright smile spread across my sister's face.

"That's a strange birthday present, Iris."

Iris just shrugs and pulls me around in a circle with her. "You know what else I want for my birthday?"

"What?"

"To dance!" she yells as pulls me back onto the dance floor.

Kieran

I was watching from the shadows when I saw Trent creep up to Avalina at the club, his intent written plainly on his face. Stalking forward from the corner I was leaning against, rage bubbling in my veins, I couldn't help the pride that sparked in my heart at watching Lina unleash her claws on the creep.

Despite knowing she could handle herself, I still felt a swell of satisfaction as my fist met flesh, the sickening crunch of bone informing me I finally broke Trent's nose.

My little chat with Trent was happening back at one of my warehouses, where I dragged his sorry ass after I knocked him out cold in the club's back lot.

Breathing in, I look down at Trent, satisfaction filling every pore of my being at the state of the loser.

The poor bastard's face was smeared with blood, which was diluted by the tears that started as soon as Trent realized, through his drunken haze, who I was and what he had done. He didn't even need me to say it. He knew.

He touched what was mine.

A growl ripped free of my throat at the thought, and I snarled as I picked up Trent's shaking body so he could face me. Even if he probably couldn't truly *see* me, the flesh around his eyes too swollen and discolored for that.

"What am I going to do with you, Trent?" I rumbled, shaking him. "I should fucking kill you."

"Please, no, I'll do anything."

"You touched what's mine, Trent."

"I didn't know! I'm sorry, man. Please, don't hurt me anymore."

I laughed, the sound bouncing off the warehouse walls. Tossing Trent to the ground like the garbage he is, I ignore his moaning. Nothing he could say would change what's about to happen.

I've been fantasizing about this moment ever since he touched Avalina in the club.

Walking over to a workbench with an assortment of hammers, nails, and rope, I pick up the blowtorch and slowly prowl over to the cowering ball of a man on the hard concrete floor.

"Don't you know? We're just getting started."

I delight in the screams that rent the air before Trent passes out. His flesh now burned where his fingers touched Avalina. He was lucky I didn't cut them off.

At least this way, he'll always have the reminder to not touch things he doesn't have permission to.

Chapter 22

AVALINA

I wake in the middle of the night to a figure looming above me, my sleep haze burning away as terror tries to outrun the scream lodged in my throat.

"Shh, Lina, it's just me." Kieran's husky timber chases away the shadows, and as he moves I can make out his piercing gaze shining in the dark.

"What are you doing here?" I rasp, my throat still working past the terror caught in its maw.

"I wanted to make sure you got home alright."

"But how did you get *in* here?"

Kieran blinks. "I have a key to your apartment."

Of course he does. I should have known. I don't have time to think through that before Kieran is moving the blankets and climbing into my bed. It's then that I notice he isn't wearing a stitch of clothing.

"Where are your clothes?"

"In your washing machine. They were dirty."

Turning over to my side so I can get a better look at him, I realize that his hair is damp. "Did you take a shower?"

Kieran's forearms come to rest over his eyes. "Yes."

"Kieran. What did you do?" I sigh, then shove at him when he doesn't answer. Sitting up, I curl my legs under me, my silk night dress pooling in my lap. I refuse to let Kieran ignore me.

Finally he relents. "Less than he deserved." Kieran moves his arms and looks at me, and I can see the fury banked there from my encounter with the drunk in the club. The intensity there is almost enough to sweep me away, to lure me into my deepest desires that only the man in front of me seems to bring out. But the connection is severed when Kieran continues. "I didn't kill him, if that's what you're asking."

"Kieran!"

"What? I thought that's what you wanted. For me to not kill him."

"Well, yes, of course I didn't want you to kill him." I shove a hand through my hair, exasperated. It's like talking to a child. "But you didn't *need* to do anything. I had it handled. He was just a drunk stranger."

"If you truly believe that, then I don't think you know me that well." Kieran sits up, muscles bunching with the movement. He rakes his heated gaze over my body. "Maybe you need a reminder."

"No, I think you need a lesson in socially acceptable behaviors. You were raised by wolves."

He smirks at the comparison. "A wolf that's going to eat you."

I scoff, frustrated by how differently he sees the situation. I try to come up with a retort, an explanation that will help him understand, but suddenly he's there, grabbing my arms and yanking me towards him, a tether I can't outrun.

With a growl, he tosses me facedown onto the silky sheets, my mind scrambling with the sudden movement. Before I can process what's happened, he's behind me, pressing his hips against mine as he pins my arms above my head in an iron grip. Leaning down his stubbled jaw scraps my cheek. "You think I'm a monster because I'd kill for you?" he whispers.

"No," I croak under his punishing hold, "Not a monster. Just misguided." I attempt to lift my head, but it's in vain as he shifts his grip on my wrists to release a hand that gathers my hair and shoves my face down as he snarls in my ear.

It's then that I realize perhaps Kieran is right. He is a monster. One who's frayed control has splintered under the weight of his code.

His hips snap against mine once again, demanding in their weight. Pleasure snakes along my spine, offering me a moment of clarity in the sea of my mind. We may not be looking at each other right now, but I know in the marrow of my bones that this is Kieran wanting me to *see* him.

I'm proven right when he rasps as his weight presses against me once more.

"I've been holding back on you, Lina. Not anymore. Do you remember your safe word?" He snarls as he lifts his hand on my head so I can answer.

"Yes." I rasp, ecstasy sparking in my veins as I attempt to move against him and chase the building pleasure.

His free hand slides under my night dress, gripping my hips and lifting them as he shifts his legs to hold mine in place. I'm trapped, held by his hand bound around my wrists and his legs anchoring mine as he slips his hand under my underwear, immediately seeking my slicked core before tracing up to my hardened nub, circling it.

His hand moves away just as my eyes begin to close by the weight of my own desire. Turning my head, I see Kieran lifting his hand to his mouth, licking his fingers with a wolfish gleam in his eyes. The sight would bring me to my knees if I wasn't already held immobile, caught in Kieran's snare. Desire flares, hot and bright, and I do my best to bank it, deciding to wait and see what Kieran will do next.

My patience is rewarded as Kieran shoves his hand inside my underwear again, pressing his thumb against my clit as two of his fingers spear me. I can't control my gasp at the sudden invasion, my walls clenching tight around the welcome intrusion. My body tries to buck and shift, to ride his fingers, but he is an immovable force. The only pleasure I find is what he gives me.

I try to be still, but soon I'm writhing and all at once Kieran's hand pulls back. Moaning, I struggle in his grasp, seeking the heat of his hand once more. Above me, Kieran chuckles as he begins to trace the outline of my underwear, my breaths becoming pants as I mentally will him to put his hand back at my clenching core, desperate to wait out this game of cat and mouse.

"Kieran, please..." The plea breaks past my clenched teeth.

In response, Kieran just rocks his hips against mine, a clear reminder that he is in charge, no matter how much I beg.

"Please, what?"

"Fuck me," I sob, "Make me come."

"Are you sure you want to be fucked by a monster?"

I growl at that, whipping my head back to meet Kieran's piercing gaze as I bare my teeth. "I don't think that. I've *never* thought that."

Kieran grips my hips, flipping me onto my back, and his lips come crashing down against mine. It's a kiss of desperation and salvation, of seeking the wildness that echoes in me as surely as it races through him.

I latch onto him, wrapping my arms and legs into a snare of my own so he can't run away. My fingernails graze his back, their bruising bite shifting into claws as Kieran lines his hips up with mine and slams into me. My back arches and Kieran's head descends to my breast, sucking a nipple into his mouth before biting. I buck against him, lost to the pressure building, to the sensation of stretching fullness as my core quivers around his cock.

We're both mindless now, rocking into each other with a snarling symphony, seeking the release that can only be found with each other.

The wave I'm riding finally crests, and I shatter as Kieran relentlessly pounds into me, stars bursting behind my closed eyelids. Kieran's breath is hot on my ear and I hear his sharp inhale before he is chasing me down the tumbling abyss of his own release.

Chapter 23

Avalina

My phone rings, the shrill sound cutting through the quiet morning. I glance at the display to see it is a call from Sarah. It's early and one of my day's off, so alarms ring in my head at the sight of Sarah's name lighting up the screen. Adrenaline courses through me, and I fumble with the phone, almost dropping it in my haste to answer.

"Sarah? Is everything okay?" I rush out, almost tripping over my words.

A chuckle answers me. "Everything is fine, Avalina. I just wanted to let you know that Mavis is at the hospital and in labor. She was at the library with me when she started having contractions. But no need to rush over here, the doctor's say it could be a few hours still. They're still in the early stages."

A shudder of relief washes through me. "Oh, thank goodness. I was so startled when you called, I almost dropped the phone, thinking something horrible had happened."

Worry laced Sarah's voice. "I'm sorry, Avalina. I didn't mean to worry you. Just thought you'd want to know."

"Of course! Yes, I definitely want to know and I'm so grateful you called. Should I bring anything? I can bring coffee or breakfast on my way in."

"I don't think my nerves can handle food right now, but coffee sounds great."

"You got it. I'll see you soon, Sarah. Give Mavis my love."

I hung up, excited about this new journey Mavis was on, but also afraid of what could happen. My accident never left me far from the idea that you never knew what was around the next bend.

Arriving at the hospital with coffee and pastries in tow, I walk through the maternity ward, surrounded by the sounds of folks in various stages of labor, and I quickly make my way to Mavis's room. The pale-colored walls contrasting with the nurses in their bright pink and green scrubs.

Greeting Sarah, I hand her the coffee and snacks so I can give Mavis a giant hug. Despite what Sarah said on the phone earlier, Mavis is clearly uncomfortable, and I do what I can do to distract my friend and keep her at ease.

"Have you heard the story of Macha?" I ask as I sit in a chair next to the bed.

Mavis lets out a pained laugh. "No, who's that?"

"She was a goddess of Ireland, who took a human lover. Her one rule for her husband, Cruinniuc, was that he was not allowed to tell anyone about her. One day he went to a festival put on by the King of Ulster, where Cruinniuc couldn't stop himself from boasting that his wife could outrun the King's fastest horses."

Mavis grimaced. "Who says things like that?"

"I know! Some folks just can't handle someone else having more power than them. And of course, the King demanded that Cruinniuc prove his claim, so his very pregnant wife was brought to the festival and forced to race against the steeds."

"She had to race against horses? While pregnant?! This story seems awful. Please tell me she at least won."

"Of course, she won! And she also gave birth to twin boys just as she crossed the finish line."

"Ouch."

"But it gets better! Remember, Macha was a goddess, and her husband did not do the one thing she required of him. So, she laid a curse on all the men of Ulster, that during the time of their greatest need, they would be stricken with the pain of childbirth for nine days."

"HA! Serves them right. I like that story."

"I thought you might."

A knock on the door announces the doctor's return to Mavis's room to check on her progress, and I quickly excuse myself to go to work. Thoughts of Mavis and her baby consume my mind as I drive to the library.

I park in my usual spot and walk towards the entrance, feeling a mix of anticipation and nervousness. As I head to the circulation desk, I note how quiet the library is today. No doubt folks are taking advantage of the warmer weather today, as they are going to be few and far between as we get deeper into fall and closer to winter.

A buzz in my pocket had me glancing at my phone to see a text from Kieran.

> *I heard about Mavis. How is she doing?*

> *How did you hear about Mavis?*

> *I hear about everything, Lina. ;)*

My eyes roll at this, and I chuckle. I know Kieran's family is powerful, but sometimes I forget what that means.

> *I even know you just rolled your eyes.*

> *There is no way you know that! :P*

> *I was wondering if you'd be up for dinner out tonight, since our last dinner date got interrupted.*

> *I didn't mind the interruption.*

There's no response for a moment, then I see the tiny bubbles appear that mean Kieran is typing a message back to me.

> *Say yes to dinner and I'll give you want you want after dinner. If you're a good girl.*

Thankfully, there aren't patrons nearby to witness the scarlet climb up my neck and face like the sunrise at dawn. I tell Kieran yes to dinner.

A s the sun descends beyond the horizon, casting a tapestry of vibrant oranges and pinks across the sky, I walk hand in hand with Kieran through the bustling streets of the city. The evening feels full of possibilities, made happier with the news I received just before Kieran picked me up that Mavis and her son, Dennis, are doing well. I make a mental note to see if the new family needs help with meals.

Kieran leads me to a hidden gem tucked away in a cobblestone alleyway, adorned with cascades of ivy that frame the entrance. The quaint restaurant exudes an old-world charm, with flickering candles casting a warm glow upon antique wooden tables draped in crisp linens.

We settle into a cozy corner booth, secluded from prying eyes.

Perusing the menu, I frown when an unexpected chill fills the air. I can't shake the feeling that something is amiss, as if the universe itself held its breath in anticipation. I try to dismiss the unease, but it stands there, just over my shoulder, haunting me.

Looking up through my lashes at Kieran, I watch as his face morphs into a stranger, as if all the warmth is leached away from his body and into the floor, disappearing like it was never there to begin with. His face is a stony mask I can't read.

I'm about to glance over my shoulder when a subtle shake of Kieran's head keeps me looking at the menu instead, even as a shadow eclipses our table, now only lit by the sole candle on top.

I don't dare glance up at the man standing near me, but I spot his large fists, scarred with age and use. What I can see from the corner of my eye has my alarm bells ringing, and I know in my bones that this is an enemy of Kieran's and not a friend.

A chuckle rumbles above me. "Well, well, if it isn't Kieran Calder. And who is this lovely lady?"

"What do you want, O'Neil?" Kieran's words are a harsh line, drawn in the sand.

"Just saying hello. Us bosses have to stick together, you know."

Suddenly a hand is under my chin, lifting my green eyes to look up into harsh blue ones. Before I can register the motion, Kieran is out of his seat, one arm on Sean O'Neil's and the other hidden from my view. My guess is the hidden hand is holding a gun to Sean's side.

"Hands off, O'Neil." Kieran snarls.

Sean chuckles again, raising his hands in mock innocence. "No harm meant, Calder. Just wanted to see if the rumors were true and that you were dating Avalina Hartwell."

Kieran growls low in his throat and Sean tries to step away, despite Kieran's grip on him. Kieran steps closer into Sean's space and whispers something in his ear before the older man turns and walks away, but not before glancing over his shoulder at me. "Be sure to have a safe drive home."

Grabbing a glass of water from the table, I take large gulps, my throat suddenly parched and tight. Anxiety rolls through me like a restless wave I have no way of fighting.

Finding my voice, I ask, "What was that?"

Kieran's mouth is set tight, but he answers me. "A threat." He reaches his hands across the table to engulf mine, an anchor that keeps me from drowning in this sea of doubt. "But I will keep you safe, Avalina. Always."

I nod, trusting Kieran at his word, despite the unease still rolling through me.

Even though I don't say anything, Kieran reads the nervousness in my sunken, withdrawn posture. Motioning to the waiter, he changes our order to-go, and I've never been more grateful to get out of the spotlight than I am now. It feels like all eyes in the restaurant are on us, the pricking sensation of whispers directed my way shivering down my spine.

The drive from the restaurant to Kieran's penthouse is silent, but full of grasping hands and reassuring caresses. I know that Kieran's lack of words isn't because of me, but more his anger at O'Neil. His posture is tight as he enters his apartment, his body an arrow ready to take flight. Probably directly into Sean O'Neil's eye.

His voice is gruff when he speaks up. "I'm sorry about tonight."

Glancing over, I frown. "You have nothing to be sorry for. O'Neil is an ass who got exactly what he wanted. A scene and under your skin."

Surprise washes across Kieran's face as he swipes a hand through his hair, his locks falling to shadow his eyes. "You're right." He comes up behind me, wrapping his arms around me and pulling me close to his chest. "It's something he's good at."

I turn so I'm facing Kieran and tilt my head up at him as I run my hands across the front of his dress shirt, silky under my fingers. "Maybe I can help you focus on something else," I murmur as I reach up to grab his hair and pull his lips down to mine.

Kieran immediately follows my lead and soon I'm backed up against the wall, Kieran nipping at my lips.

I lightly shove at his shoulders, and Kieran obeys, backing up while I unbutton his shirt and moving to untuck it from his pants.

A huff sounds above my head and then Kieran's hands are over mine, grabbing his shirt and ripping it away. Glancing up, I arch an eyebrow at Kieran's smirk, satisfaction purring in my veins as it fades away once I undo his belt and unzip his pants.

Sinking to my knees, I untuck Kieran's cock and lick the underside of his shaft, watching Kieran's eyes darken the color of the earth after a hard rain.

Hissing through his teeth, Kieran's hands thread through my hair as I swallow his length, pulling back as I gag on his girth.

"We can't have that, now, can we?" Kieran's voice is smoke and steel—rough and demanding, a blade to cut myself on.

I gasp as Kieran's hands grip my tresses tighter. "You want to give me something else to think about, Lina? Let me watch you choke like a good girl."

He shoves his way down my throat, demanding access as I try to breathe past the panic and through my nose. The idea of not being able to inhale much worse than the reality truly is.

I can't stop my gag as Kieran pushes me just past a pace I'm comfortable with, his clasp on my head holding me in place while his hips piston his cock up and down my throat.

"Fuck, you're perfect," Kieran rasps as he watches the tears falling down my face as I sputter around him.

His hands shift from my hair to under my arms, and suddenly I'm lifting on my feet, Kieran licking away the salt and saliva from my face. "Hands against the wall, Lina."

I turn to do as he asked, bracing myself as my clothes are ripped away and suddenly Kieran is there, pressing the head of his cock at my entrance, already soaked and wanting.

"So fucking needy, this cunt," he grows as he shoves inside in one thrust, his hands on my hips the only thing keeping me upright as euphoria races through me, heedless of anything in its path.

The pleasure swirls and rises, building with each delicious stroke. Bliss short-circuits my brain as my body writhes under Kieran's powerful frame.

My back arches even more as Kieran grazes his teeth along my neck before biting down, marking my body like he's marked my soul.

Chapter 24

AVALINA

The city lights flooded the sky and blotted out the stars. I can't see any trees from Kieran's penthouse, only buildings and artificial light, such a difference from my apartment that backs up against the forest. The location of our homes isn't the only thing that is different. While my home is all muted colors and light wood, Kieran favors deep mahogany and leather. His home is spacious and full of windows, allowing him to see the world he rules.

Sipping the now lukewarm coffee, I stifle a yawn. I am doing my best to stay awake until Kieran gets home, even though he told me I didn't need to. He's been working a lot of late nights lately, trying to tie up loose ends to corner Sean, allowing Finn to take over the O'Neils once and for all.

I'm currently sitting outside on the penthouse balcony, swept away by a book, and wrapped in blankets to ward off the late autumn chill. I can't see many stars here because of the city lights, but the city itself was like a kaleidoscope of stars themselves.

Looking at my watch, I sigh, seeing that it was nearing midnight. I need to go to sleep, as I have the morning shift at the library tomorrow. I gather my things and make my way back inside the penthouse, returning the book back to its shelf.

Kieran wasn't lying when he told me he liked to read, as he had more books than I did, all resting on bookcases stretched throughout his living space. I run my hand over the spines, an assortment of book cloth, paper, and leather covering the tomes. I like to think that they, too, were silently waiting for Kieran's return. If I think of it like that, I don't feel so alone in this space that is surrounded by the bustling city. Even though my apartment is on the outskirts of town, I prefer it's quiet nature to the constant roar of the city streets below.

Taking one last look back at the dark and quiet space, I softly pad to the bedroom to get some much-needed sleep. A part of me wants to worry that Kieran isn't home yet, but I know he can handle himself. He wouldn't be where he is if he couldn't deal with the things that go bump in the night.

Sitting up in terror, a scream catches in my throat and my heart races to escape an invisible predator. I thrash under the weight of the blanket, feeling trapped by a cage of sharp metal and twisted steel.

Instantly, Kieran is up as well, turning to me and grabbing my shoulders.

"Lina, what's wrong? What is it?"

I feel frozen. Stuck. A fish on dry land gasping for air that can never reach my lungs.

Worry snakes its way across Kieran's features, illuminated by the soft moonlight shining through his bedroom windows.

Nodding as I suck in lungfuls of air, I grab Kieran's hands, hoping he can understand what I am wordlessly trying to say.

Kieran's brow furrows. "Nightmare?"

I nod again.

Large hands gently move me, pulling my shaking limbs into a bundle of blankets and a firm embrace. The echo of steel embedded in my skin fades as the heat of Kieran's body against mine grounds me in the present moment.

After a moment, Kieran tilts my chin up, so I'm looking into his dark, mahogany eyes.

"What gives you nightmares, Avalina?" His gaze is soft, but Kieran can't hide the bite of his words that are as sharp as knives.

Despite his gruff delivery, I know Kieran isn't angry at me. How can he be when his hands hold me like I am his last breath?

Inhaling his whisky and smoke scent to ground me, I let my mask fall and tell Kieran of the nightmares that have plagued me ever since I woke up in the hospital after the accident.

Words spill out of my mouth like petals falling in the rain as I describe the memories that wake me at night. Memories of groaning metal collapsing around me, crushing and slicing as I'm tossed carelessly among glass and thorns by the lake edge.

Kieran listens silently, but there's no mistaking the tension he holds in the taut lines of his body, so carefully caging mine.

"You've had these since the accident?"

"Yes. They aren't as bad now, though. I haven't had one in weeks. They used to happen every night, and I'd have to get up and take a shower and change my sheets because I would wake up drenched in sweat. The nightmares feel so real." I look up from my ramblings to see Kieran scowl and I frown. He catches it and places a soft kiss on my lips.

"I'm not mad at you. I'm mad at the person responsible for the accident. Responsible for hurting you. For still hurting you."

"Have you found anything out about who caused it?"

"No, but Cass is looking into it. If there is anything we missed before, any stone we left unturned, she'll discover it."

I snuggle in closer to Kieran, craving his heat, his flesh against mine. A reminder that I'm not alone and tumbling about in the wreckage that sliced open my soul. Kieran's arms wrap around me, pulling the covers back over my body.

"Go back to sleep, Lina. I'll keep watch," his voice rumbles with my ear pressed to his chest. I want to protest, to tell him I'm fine, that I don't need him protecting me from the shadows, but something makes me pause. This is Kieran, the one person who has never made me feel less than for my missing memories, who refuses to let me apologize when I realize he's talking about something I've forgotten. The realization that I'm utterly safe here with him settles over my bones and I let my eyelids close, knowing I won't have any more nightmares tonight.

Chapter 25

Kieran

I am stewing, wondering about the danger I am putting Avalina in by starting up our relationship again. My heart wants to sing from the rooftops, but my mind doesn't trust this feeling, doesn't trust this hope.

Despite the desire to go legit, that doesn't erase the danger that comes with being associated with me, with my family. A knock interrupts my torment. I straighten, smoothing my features into an impassive mask.

"Enter," I command, my voice betraying none of the war burning within me. There is work to be done. And I will do it, no matter how my traitorous heart railed against the confines of duty.

She will be protected, even from myself.

The door opens and Cassie enters, her lithe form gliding across the room to stand before my desk. As always, her gaze is direct and assessing.

"You wanted to see me?" she asks, though we both know why she is here. Cassandra is my second, privy to all my secrets. Including those I wished desperately to deny.

"What did you find out?" I ask bluntly, resisting the urge to pour myself another drink. I need all my wits for this conversation.

Cassie hesitates, just for a moment. But it is enough. Dread curdles in my stomach even before she speaks.

"It was one of Sean's men," she says quietly. "That cut the brake lines on Avalina's car that night."

I close my eyes as her words slam into me. My hands curl into fists against the desk.

"Are you certain?" I grind out behind clenched teeth. But of course she is. Cassandra would not have come to me unless she was absolutely sure.

"Yes. The accident was meant for you. They thought you were with her that night."

Sean had almost killed the girl I... cared for. Avalina could have died that night. Because of this stupid war with O'Neil.

Crimson, fiery rage surges through me, and it is only through sheer force of will that I leash it. Later, I would deal with my Sean. But now, I had to ensure Avalina's safety.

Opening my eyes, I meet Cassandra's gaze. "How did Sean find out?"

Cass shrugs. "Originally, you weren't as careful as you thought. One of Sean's men saw you with her at Kingsdale Park and Sean started having her followed. They realized you were together."

"And now?"

"You've been putting pressure on Sean and that's keeping him busy, buying you time. But he is bound to know you two are back together, especially after that *very* public stunt you pulled at the gala."

The feeling I was trying to avoid earlier, the waiting that things were bound to go wrong between Avalina and me...it's staring me in the face now and I can't look away.

"I put her in danger once. I won't do it again."

Cassandra nods. We both understand there is only one way to protect Avalina now. I have to let her go.

I take a deep breath, steadying myself. This was the only way I knew. No matter how much it would hurt us both.

"I'll end things with her," I mumble. "Make her believe I've lost interest."

Cassandra's eyes widen. "Kieran, are you sure? I know how you feel about her."

A muscle ticks in my jaw. She is right, damn her. My feelings for Avalina have grown far past mere intrigue. But it doesn't matter now.

"It's the only way to keep her safe. If she stays close to me, to my family..." I trail off. The threat is obvious. As long as she is tied to us, she is in danger.

Cassandra nods reluctantly. "Just...you'll have to do it publicly. To keep her safe, you'll have to hurt her where Sean can see." She quietly makes her way out the door.

I turn away, not wanting her to see the pain in my eyes. Hurt Avalina? It will destroy me. But I have no choice.

I thought of her smile, so open and warm. Of the light in her eyes when she looked my way. Could I really extinguish that light forever?

My hands curl into fists again. I have to. For her sake.

Squaring my shoulders, I cage my heart. I will do what I have to protect her, no matter the cost. Even if it means sacrificing my chance at happiness.

I take a deep breath, the familiar scent of leather and mahogany grounding me. But there is no comfort to be found within these walls tonight.

I move to the window and look out at the moonlit grounds below. Somewhere out there, Avalina slept, blissfully unaware of the danger I hope to keep at bay.

Avalina will remain safe, even if it means my ruin.

Chapter 26

Kieran

My heart feels like a stone sinking in the depths of an ocean, pulled down by the gravity of my love for Avalina and the iron chains of duty that bind me to my family. I've spent countless restless nights wrestling with my thoughts, torn between keeping the woman who haunts my dreams by my side, but also ensuring her safety. My conclusion is that I can't do both.

The burnished glow of the setting sun drapes over Avalina's shoulder-length hair, turning it into a cascade of molten copper. As we approach the restaurant, I feel the familiar prickling awareness—the sensation of unseen eyes tracing my movements with lethal precision.

"Mandolin" reads the brass sign hanging above the door, swinging gently in the evening breeze. It's a popular spot, revered for its culinary excellence and romantic ambiance. Yet, beneath the veneer of sophistication lies a truth only I am privy to: this place is a puppet on Sean O'Neil's malevolent strings.

"Kieran, this place looks incredible," Avalina breathes out, her green eyes reflecting the warm light that spills from the windows onto the cobbled street.

I can't help but study her face—the serene composure that makes her all the more alluring in her ignorance of the dark undercurrents swirling around us. She's rediscovered herself since the accident, and I've been captivated by her rebirth, her passion for life that blooms like a rare flower in adversity's soil. But she doesn't remember the secret we once shared, or the danger that now shadows her steps.

"Trust me, it's not half as incredible as you," I murmur, ensuring every word drips with the truth of my desire. The iron knot of dread tightens in my stomach, knowing what I have to do tonight.

We're seated at a secluded table, draped in white linen and adorned with a single crimson rose. The scent of garlic and red wine mingles in the air, teasing the senses, creating an illusion of normalcy that I am about to shatter.

"Kieran?" Avalina's voice cuts through the din of clinking glasses and subdued conversations, pulling me back from the precipice of my brooding thoughts.

I take a deep breath and let it out slowly, feeling the weight of my decision crush me with its finality. "Avalina, there's something I need to tell you."

She leans forward, concern etching her delicate features, and I brace myself against the wave of emotion her proximity evokes.

Taking a breath, I force the damning words past my lips. "Sean... he was behind your accident," I confess, the words bitter on my tongue, acid to my pride that I can't keep Avalina safe, then or now. Her eyes widen in shock, a silent question forming on her lips.

"It was meant for me," I continue, forcing myself to maintain eye contact, to lay bare the ugliness that taints our reality. "He wanted to get to me, and you... you were collateral damage."

I ran my hands through my hair. "But I wasn't in the car. The fact that you couldn't remember our relationship seemed to satisfy Sean, since as far as I can tell, he hasn't tried anything since."

Turning towards her, I take Avalina's hands in my own, staring into her emerald green eyes. "But Lina, as long as you're with me, you have a target on your head. I wouldn't be able to live with myself if something happened to you."

I watch the realization dawn in her eyes, the horror and disbelief that flickers across her face before settling into a heart-wrenching vulnerability.

"Because of that, we can't be together," I say, each syllable laced with the agony of renunciation. "I won't—I can't—put you in danger again."

The candlelight between us flickers, casting shadows that play upon her features, accentuating the soft curve of her cheeks and the gentle bow of her lips—lips I've yearned to taste since the moment she forgot me.

My hand trembles slightly as I toss a few crisp bills onto the table, more than enough to cover the untouched meal and the silence that's settled between us like a thick fog. Avalina's voice rises in a crescendo of desperation and disbelief, her words clawing at me, begging me to reconsider.

"But I don't fear that, Kieran. You keep me safe."

"Don't you see?" I yell. "I didn't keep you safe. I almost got you killed!"

Shame slams into me, hot and hard, at the flinch that flashes across Avalina's face. I bury my face in my hands, drowning in an ocean of guilt and sorrow that pierces my soul. Delicate hands curl around my own scared ones, pulling them down into my lap as determined eyes meet my own.

"You can't control Sean, Kieran. The accident wasn't your fault."

I go to argue, but she cuts me off. "No, I won't let you take the blame."

Hesitating, I cup her face. "If anything happened to you..." I trail off, ice flooding my veins at the thought. "Lina, I... my life ends when yours does. It's as simple as that. I know you don't want to hear it, but this has to be the end."

"I don't believe you."

"I'm serious, Lina. I'll do anything I have to if it means keeping you safe."

"You've already decided, haven't you? You've made your mind up and it doesn't matter what I say."

"Kieran, please—"

But my resolve is ironclad, reinforced by the knowledge of what could happen if I allow my heart to rule over my head. It's a battle, every instinct screaming to pull her close, to shield her from the cruel world with my own body. But Sean's shadows lurk in every corner, and I can't—won't—be the reason she falls prey to them again.

"Listen to me," I interrupt, the edge in my voice cutting through her pleas. "This isn't up for discussion. It's not safe."

Her green eyes glisten, those emerald pools where I once found solace now reflecting only pain and confusion. Her lips part, but it's her soul that seems to shatter, the soundless echo of her heart fracturing beneath the weight of my withdrawal. I watch silently as the tears gather in Avalina's eyes, silently falling down her pale cheeks.

The knife that was currently slicing my heart into ribbons twists as I rise from the chair, the legs scraping against the floor with a harshness screech. The space between us becomes a chasm too perilous to cross. I turn my back on her sobs, each one a lash against the remnants of my composure, branding me with guilt and longing.

"Take care of yourself, Avalina," I murmur, low enough that it's carried away by the murmurs of the oblivious diners around us.

My steps are heavy, weighted by the burden of decisions made in the darkness—a darkness that clings to me, even as I step into the cool night air.

Behind me, Avalina's grief fills the room, a haunting melody that threatens to drag me back. But I cannot falter; I cannot fall.

*A*valina

Tears stream down my face unchecked, salt tracing the outline of my lips—a bitter reminder of the taste of Kieran's kiss that I yearn for but may never experience again. The fabric of the plush chair feels alien under my fingertips, a stark contrast to the warmth of his touch that had promised so much more.

"Shh, Avie, let's get you home," Claire's voice is soft, yet it cuts through the haze of my misery. She slides into the seat Kieran vacated, her presence a pale substitute for the man whose absence has hollowed out my chest.

"Claire? What are you doing here?" I ask between gasping breaths, trying to calm my racing heart, to stop the tears that keep flowing.

"Kieran called me." Claire swallows, sighs. "He told me it was too dangerous for you two to be together, that he was going to end it and wanted me to make sure you got home okay."

I nod mutely, unable to articulate the storm raging within. Claire wraps an arm around my shoulders, guiding me up and out of the booth. With each step, the remnants of my shattered poise crumble, leaving a trail of sorrow in our wake as we exit the restaurant.

The night air is a slap against my wet cheeks, and I shiver—not from the cold, but from the sudden exposure to a world that feels less familiar without him by my side. Claire's car awaits us, a silent sentinel in the dimly lit parking lot.

"Come on, sweetheart," Claire coaxes, her tone gentle. "Let's go home."

But 'home' is just another word for a place where the echoes of Kieran's goodbye will resonate through empty rooms and sleepless nights—an abode turned mausoleum for a love that was as intoxicating as it was forbidden.

Chapter 27

Avalina

The sun peeks through my curtains, stirring me from restless sleep. An uneasy feeling settles in the pit of my stomach as memories of Kieran flash through my mind. His piercing umber eyes. The warmth of his embrace. The husky timbre of his voice whispering my name.

I reach for my phone, fingers trembling. Countless unanswered calls and messages left on read. I still can't believe Kieran's ignoring me. I wasn't sure when he made his declaration that he was really letting go, but it had been days of no answer. We were so close just last week, bodies and souls intertwined in passion. Now there is only silence. A hollow ache fills my chest, squeezing the breath from my lungs.

I call him again, listening to the dull ring that signals his rejection. When his voicemail picks up, I can't find the words. The line goes dead. My chest tightens, the ache of uncertainty spreading like ink through water.

Defeated, I curl into a ball under the covers, Kieran's scent of whiskey and smoke clinging to my pillow. The memories come unbidden, a chaotic swirl of emotion. His hands roaming my body. Lips tasting every inch of bare skin.

A single tear escapes my eye, tracing a path along my cheek. As if it were a lifeline, I grasp onto the clarity it brings. The cold reality that love alone can't dispel the shadows that exist in Kieran's life.

The ache inside intensifies, threatening to consume me whole. I cling to the fading hope that Kieran will come back to me. That he will make everything right again.

Until then, I am adrift in a sea of sorrow, longing for the man who holds my heart. The man who is slipping further away with each passing day. The man I fear I may lose forever.

A knock sounds on my bedroom door and I look up to see Claire carrying a tray of tea and cookies.

"Morning, Avie," she says, her voice low and soothing. She sets the tray down on the nightstand and sits on the edge of my bed. "I thought you might need this."

I can feel my face crumbling, and Claire envelops me in a warm hug. I melt into her embrace, the dam breaking once more, as tears stream down my face. Claire murmurs soothing words, stroking my hair until the sobs subside.

"Thanks," I mutter, the word barely able to navigate the tightness in my throat. Claire picks up a steaming cup of tea and hands it to me.

The warmth from the cup seeps into my palms, a stark contrast to the cold desolation gripping my heart.

"Drink up," Claire encourages, her own blue eyes brimming with unshed tears for my pain. "And maybe a hot shower will help?"

Nodding numbly, I sip the sweetened tea, the floral notes of lemon balm attempting to calm the storm raging inside me. The cookies are untouched; I have no appetite for anything other than the answers that evade me.

There's a fluttering at the pit of my stomach when the doorbell rings. Iris. Her energy breezes in before she does, a tempest of concern and sisterly love. Yet behind the worry lines on her brow, there's something else—a relief that doesn't quite sit right with me.

"Hey, Avie," Iris greets me, pulling me into a hug that's a little too enthusiastic. "You're going to be okay, you know that? Better off, really."

Her words sting, the implication clear. She never approved of Kieran, always saw him as a shadow lurking in my sunlit world. But she doesn't understand the magnetic pull he has on me, the undeniable connection that lingers even now.

"Thanks, Iris," I reply, my voice hollow. How can they see it as so black and white when my soul is painted in shades of him?

"Come on, Avalina, let the water wash away some of the hurt," Claire suggests again, gently steering me toward the bathroom and away from my sister.

With each step, I feel the weight of their love trying to anchor me back to reality. But as the steam from the shower begins to rise, all I can think of is the last time Kieran and I were enveloped in mist together, our bodies entwined, lost in a dance of desire and whispered promises. Now, I'm left swaying alone, grappling with a melody that has been abruptly silenced.

The tendrils of steam fade into the air, taking with them the ghost of his touch that I can still feel lingering on my skin. Water droplets cling to me like the remnants of a dream I'm not ready to wake from. Wrapped in a towel, the fabric rough against my tender heart, I step back into my room, where reality awaits.

"Better?" Claire's voice is soft, laced with concern as her eyes search mine for any sign of the girl she once knew.

I manage a nod, though it feels like lying. "A little."

"Come sit," she coaxes, patting the spot beside her on the bed, and I obey, the heaviness in my limbs making each movement an effort. The bed dips under our weight, and she hands me a new mug of tea, the scent of chamomile rising in the air, a subtle invitation to calm.

"Talk to me, Ava." Her hand finds mine, fingers gentle yet insistent.

"Every part of me just...aches, Claire." My voice is a mere whisper, betraying the turmoil within. "It's like he's still everywhere—his voice, his scent, the warmth of his skin..."

"Memories have a way of holding us hostage," she says, and I wonder how she can possibly understand this searing pain that threatens to consume me.

"Will it ever stop hurting?"

Claire's thumb strokes the back of my hand, a soothing rhythm that anchors me to the here and now. "It will," she assures me, her conviction a lifeline thrown into the turbulent sea of my sorrow. "But you have to give yourself permission to let go first."

"Letting go feels like losing him all over again," I admit, the confession pulling at the stitches of my wounded soul.

"I know," Claire sighs. "Which is why you need to focus on yourself right now. Take time to heal and find your own happiness again." Her lips curve into a soft smile. "I bet you'll feel better once you get back to work on Monday. Immerse yourself in books and let their stories inspire you."

"Do you really think that will help?" I ask doubtfully.

"It's worth a try," Claire insists. " Remember who you are, Avalina. Kieran was just a chapter in your story, not the whole book."

Her words are meant to heal, but they slice through the fog of my longing with the sharpness of truth. "What if I don't know how to start the next chapter?"

"Then we'll find it together." Claire's promise is fierce, an oath sworn by the steadfast heart of friendship. "You're not alone, Ava. You never have been."

Chapter 28

AVALINA

The thrill of anticipation courses through my veins like a wild, untamed river. Claire has meticulously planned tonight—a girls' night out meant to lift my spirits and help me reclaim some semblance of normalcy. It has been weeks since *that* night, and although my heart is still sore, I know some time out with my friends will help me leave behind the shadows that haunt my steps.

As I stand before the full-length mirror in my bedroom, I can't help but feel a nervous energy skittering beneath my skin, as if tiny sparks were igniting my every nerve. I bite my lip, considering the outfit I'd chosen for tonight.

The plunging black satin dress clung to my curves, daringly short and revealing more than it concealed. The thought of stepping out in such an attire sends shivers down my spine, and yet, I crave the exhilaration of pushing my boundaries.

I take one last look at my reflection, noting how the dress accentuates my hourglass figure and makes my copper hair shimmer like molten caramel. With a determined nod, I slip into my strappy stilettos, feeling the delicious thrill of empowerment as the heels add inches to my height.

"Deep breaths, Avalina," I whisper to myself, trying to calm my racing heart. Anxiety crawls its way through me like the branches of a rambling blackberry, heedless of the prickling of its thorns. I turn away from the mirror, grab my purse, and step out of my apartment, ready to shake off the heavy weight that had gathered the past few weeks.

The moment I emerge from my apartment building, Claire's black convertible roars into view, headlights gleaming like twin orbs in the twilight. The car comes to a halt at the curb, and Claire bounds out of the driver's seat, her blonde waves bouncing with every step.

"Girl, you look absolutely stunning!" she exclaims, drawing me into a fierce hug as if we hadn't seen each other in years. "Tonight is going to be epic. I've planned everything to perfection, down to our very own VIP booth. You deserve nothing less than the best, Avie."

I feel a surge of gratitude for my friend's thoughtfulness. Smiling, I squeeze Claire's hand. "I can't wait, Claire. Thank you for this."

Claire grins and ushers me into the passenger seat, sliding gracefully behind the wheel. "No time to waste! We have reservations at the hottest new restaurant in town, followed by an exclusive club that even celebrities have trouble getting into."

As the convertible speeds through the city, the wind whips through my hair, carrying away my lingering doubts. The night air feels charged with possibility, and I revel in it.

"Here we are," Claire announces as we pull up to an imposing glass building, its facade illuminated by blue and purple lights that shimmer like stars. The restaurant's name, "Elysium," glows in elegant silver letters above the entrance.

"Wow, Claire. This place looks amazing," I breathe, taking in the luxurious ambiance.

"Only the best for my partner in crime," Claire winks.

We enter Elysium, and I'm immediately enveloped in a world of opulence. Crystal chandeliers cast a warm glow over tables draped with crisp, white linens. Silverware gleams against fine china, and the clink of glasses mingle with the soft hum of conversation.

We're led to our table by a floor-to-ceiling window overlooking the cityscape. The view is breathtaking, mixing the city lights with the glow of the waxing moon.

Sipping on champagne and feasting on delicate flavors that dance upon our tongues, Claire and I trade stories, our laughter punctuating the night like fireworks.

"We used to sneak out at midnight just to watch the stars. Do you remember that?" I reminisce, a wistful smile playing on my lips.

"Of course! Those were some of our best memories," Claire replies, her eyes sparkling with shared nostalgia.

"Tonight reminds me of those times," I muse, "when anything seemed possible."

"Anything is still possible, Ava," Claire insists, her gaze intense. "You've come so far since your accident, and I couldn't be prouder. Tonight is about celebrating the incredible woman you are."

I felt warmth bloom in my chest, buoyed by Claire's unwavering support. "Here's to us, then," I said, raising my glass. "And to embracing the unknown."

"Cheers!" Claire echoes, clinking our glasses together.

The night unfurls like a dream, and I surrender myself to its magic as we finished up our dinner and head to the nightclub. It feels good to let my worries go, even if a part of me knows it's only temporary.

The dance floor pulses with energy beneath a sea of swirling lights. The beats vibrate through our bodies, and we move as if connected by an invisible thread, perfectly in sync with each other.

"Remember that ridiculous dance we made up when we were twelve?" I shout over the music, laughter glinting in my eyes.

Claire playfully rolls her eyes before responding, "How could I forget? We called it 'The Electric Caterpillar'!"

"Let's do it!" I insist, grinning mischievously. We exchange a knowing glance and launch into the synchronized dance we'd choreographed years ago — a wild blend of exaggerated movements and unrestrained joy.

As we dance, the rest of the world seems to fade away, leaving us in our own private universe. Even if I still wasn't as close with my other friends, I knew Claire would always be there for me.

But despite the euphoria, I can't shake the sudden chill that shivers down my spine, warning bells sounding at my unease. I glance around, but everything seems as it should be: people dancing and enjoying themselves, lost in the moment.

"Hey, are you okay?" Claire asks, concern etched on her face as she notes my distraction.

"Uh, yeah, I think so," I hesitate, trying to brush off the unsettling feeling. "It's just... I don't know. I feel like something's not right."

"Maybe we just need a break from the dance floor," Claire suggests, taking my hand and leading me to a quieter corner of the club where we could catch our breath.

"Thanks, Claire," I murmur.

"Always," Claire replies with a warm smile. "I'm parched. I'm going to get us some drinks. Maybe that will help."

"Sounds good. I'm going to step outside for a minute to get some fresh air."

"You want me to come with you?"

"No, I'll just be right outside the door. I'll be fine."

"Okay."

As I step outside onto the club's dimly lit patio, I take a deep breath, filling my lungs with the cool night air that smells of autumn leaves. I try to focus on the present moment–the laughter and conversation drifting from nearby–but can't ignore the lingering sensation that something is wrong, like whispers in the shadows just beyond my reach.

Leaning against the railing of the patio, my eyes wander to an inconspicuous corner where a group of men huddle together, their bulky figures draped in dark clothing. There is something predatory about them — like wolves stalking their prey and I can feel the hairs on my arms rise in alarm.

My fingers begin to fidget nervously, and I turn to go back inside. The air around me seems to grow colder, heavier, suffused with an oppressive malice.

"Hello, pretty girl," a gravelly voice hisses behind me, making me jump. I whip around to find one of the menacing men from across the street, his face half-hidden in shadow. The others materialize around me, closing in like vultures circling their prey.

"What are you doing?" I demand, my voice barely concealing the tremor of fear that ripples through me. "What do you want?"

"Ah, we've been watching you," the man sneers, a cruel grin twisting his lips. "You're coming with us."

"Excuse me? I don't think so!" I spit, my heart pounding wildly against my rib cage. Stepping back, I bump into one of the men, their looming forms casting sinister shadows on the pavement.

"Where's Kieran Calder when you need him, huh?" another man laughs maliciously, sending shivers down my spine. How did they know about Kieran?

"Leave him out of this!" I snarl, anger flaring within me like wildfire. "He has nothing to do with whatever messed up game you're playing!"

"Kieran means a great deal to our boss," the first man replies, his eyes glinting dangerously in the low light. "And you, my dear, are our bargaining chip."

Before I can react, rough hands grab my arms yanking me towards the alley beside the club. Terror surges through my veins, an icy torrent threatening to drown me. But as I'm dragged deeper into the darkness, I refuse to let fear consume me—I will not go down without a fight.

As they continue to drag me along, my mind races, desperately searching for a plan, a chance to break free. Then, suddenly, inspiration strikes—my stilettos. They are sharp, dangerous, and, most importantly, within reach.

"Hey," I call out with feigned sweetness, catching the captors off guard. "If you're so determined to take me somewhere, at least let me walk properly. These shoes are killing me."

"Fine," the lead crony growls, clearly annoyed by my persistence. "But don't try anything stupid."

"Wouldn't dream of it," I reply innocently, bending down to adjust my shoe. My fingers brush against the spiked heel and grip it tightly. Taking a deep breath, I steel myself for what comes next.

With a sudden burst of adrenaline-fueled strength, I swing my stiletto towards the crony's face, its pointed heel slicing through the air like a razor. The man howls in pain as blood spurts from his now-gashed cheek.

My legs move before my mind has even processed the thought, prey now attempting to outrun the predator. As the cronies stumble in shock, I sprint back toward the club, my heart pounding like thunder.

"Stop her!" the injured crony bellows, rage tinging his every word. Heavy boots pound the pavement as they close in on me.

My breath comes in ragged gasps as I run, my chest heaving with effort. The distance between me and my pursuers is closing rapidly, their malicious snarls echoing in my ears, but I don't dare look back. I know I can't outrun the wolves forever.

My legs burn as I sprint, lungs pleading for air. The crisp night wind whips across my flushed cheeks, the scent of fear and sweat mingling with the city's smoky haze. Heartbeat pounding in my ears like a drum, its rhythm syncing with the heavy footsteps that chase me.

"Stop running, sweetheart!" one of the goons taunts, his voice thick with malice. "It'll only make this harder for you!"

"Never," I whisper through gritted teeth, forcing my body to push past its breaking point. A surge of anger swells within me, igniting a primal urge to fight, to resist, to survive.

As I turn the corner, my eyes scan the dimly lit street for any sign of salvation. Desperation gnaws at my chest as every escape route seems to evaporate before my eyes.

Panic claws at my insides, threatening to unravel my resolve. And then, like a beacon in the darkness, a narrow alleyway appears up ahead.

"Please let this work," I pray silently, veering off into the shadowy passage.

"Where'd she go?" I hear one of them shout, the confusion in his voice bringing a fleeting moment of satisfaction. But I can't afford to waste time savoring it.

The alleyway was littered with obstacles: dumpsters, broken crates, and piles of trash. My legs, shaking from exhaustion, navigate the cluttered terrain despite the terror coursing through my veins.

"Where are you, sweetheart?" one of the men calls out, his predatory tone sending shivers down my spine. "Can't hide forever!"

"*Watch me*," I think, ducking behind a large dumpster as my heart threatens to break free from my chest.

Silence envelops the alleyway, broken only by the distant echo of boots on the pavement. The air is thick with tension, every nerve in my body coiled like a spring, ready to snap at any moment.

"Give it up, boys," a gruff voice growls, frustration seeping through his words. "She's long gone."

"Boss won't be happy," another mutters, the sound of their retreat gradually fading away.

I allow myself a single shaky breath, relief washing over me in waves. But as I prepare to emerge from my hiding place, a vice-like grip seizes my arm, wrenching me into the open.

"Thought you could get away from us, did you?" the crony snarls, his face twisted into a cruel grin. "We're not done with you yet."

The world around me blurs as panic consumes my senses, distorting them into a tapestry of blurry shapes and colors. Desperately, I fight against his iron grip, my fingers clawing at his skin in a futile attempt to break free.

"Let me go!" I scream, my voice raw and desperate, lungs empty from my race through the shadows. "You'll never get away with this!"

"Looks like we already have, sweetheart," he taunts, a wicked smile plastered across his face.

As the darkness of despair threatens to swallow me whole, I make one last desperate plea: "Kieran, help me"–but my voice was little more than a whisper, lost in the chilly night air.

Chapter 29

Kieran

The door slams open with a resounding thud, causing the walls to shudder. I let out a curse at the intruder, but unease catches the words in my throat as Cassandra hurries over to my desk, hair disheveled and sweaty, like she ran here.

"It's Avalina." she gasps. "He got her. Sean."

"What?" I bark, a demand more than a question.

Cass's chest heaves with exhaustion, and she bends over as she rasps out, "They ambushed her, outside of the nightclub she and Claire were at. Claire got worried when Avalina went outside to get some air and didn't return. It was clearly Sean's men on the security footage who cornered her in the alley before tossing her in the back of their SUV."

The chair under me groans beneath my hands, my fury barely leashed. "They weren't hiding."

"No, they weren't." Cass replies.

"Why go after her now? I broke it off."

"Kieran," Cass begins, hesitating for a split second before continuing, "we both know it's a trap. Sean wants to kill you for messing with his business. If you go after Avalina, you might both end up dead."

"But if I don't go," I growl, "then she will most definitely end up dead and I rather not live if that's the case."

Learning forward, I brace my arms against the cold wood of my desk, pressing my forehead against my fists as I try to steady my racing heart. The image of Avalina's vulnerable gaze haunts me like a specter I can't shake off. With every beat of my heart, the urgency of her safety becomes more palpable.

"Fuck," the curse hissed between my teeth, forcing myself to breathe in deeply. The scent of aged leather and dark mahogany fills my nostrils, grounding me momentarily. I have never been one to waver, but now my affection for Avalina is threatening to unravel me entirely.

"Kieran," Cass's voice breaks through my thoughts, her concern etched across her face. "You know this could tear everything apart."

I clench my fists, feeling the weight of responsibility and loyalty bearing down on me like a crushing force. The only way out is to kill Sean, but that may cause more turmoil in the end.

"Damn it, I know!" I growl, frustration seeping into every word. "But what choice do I have? She's in danger because of us — because of me."

I pace the room, the woven carpet beneath my dress shoes quickly bowing under the weight of my anger rolling off me in waves.

The door creaks open to reveal Liam, and he and Cass whisper back and forth with frantic gazes in my direction.

"Listen to me, brother," Liam urges, gripping my shoulder with a strength that belied his worry. "I understand your love for her, but you are risking everything we've built. Our power, our legacy, our family's very survival."

"Her life is worth more than all of that," I insist, the conviction in my words ringing true. I know that by choosing her safety over my loyalty to my family, I am potentially sacrificing everything I hold dear. But how can I live with myself if I let her die?

"No," I say firmly, my resolve unwavering. "I love her, and I will protect her at any cost."

"Even if it means destroying our hold, erasing everything we've worked for?" he asks, his voice heavy.

"Even then," I reply, my heart aching at the thought of the potential consequences. But I can not, *will not*, abandon Avalina to the darkness that threatens to consume her.

"Very well," Liam nods, understanding filling his gaze. "I'm always with you, you know that."

"Thank you," I murmur, grateful for his support, even as I know we might both pay dearly for my decision.

The wind howls like a wounded wolf, clawing its way through the narrow alleys of the city. I shiver, pulling my coat tighter around me as I stare into the darkness. There is no turning back now. My mind is made up, my heart resolute. For Avalina, I will defy my family, defy everything I have been taught since birth.

"Kieran," a gravelly voice whispers from behind me. I turn to see Finn, his face holding an emotion I can't name. "Are you certain about this?"

"More than anything," I reply, my jaw set in determination. "I can't stand by while Avalina is in danger."

Finn nods gravely, understanding the weight of my decision. He places a hand on my shoulder, offering both comfort and support. "Then let's get her back."

We gather with Cass and Liam - the only other ones I trust with this.

"Cass," I murmur, my breath fogging in the cold air. "You've gathered information; what do we know?"

"She's being held in the basement of Sean's house," she replies, her voice low and urgent. "Which means it's heavily guarded. We'll have to use force."

"But that might get Avalina killed in the process."

"We'll need help. I have a few O'Neil men I trust. They're ready to assist us when we give the signal." Finn says.

"The O'Neils are why she was taken in the first place." I snap.

Finn winces at that. "I know, but I trust these people with my life. One of them is Sloane."

"Fine," I say, my voice barely audible above the wind's mournful cry. I trust Finn, and I trust Sloane. If they say they can get help, I have to believe it.

Cass, Liam, and Finn set out planning the attack. My mind races and can't focus on anything other than the thrumming of my pulse, the urge to let my beast loose and destroy everything.

Sean thinks he set the perfect trap, a way to get me off my turf and onto his where he can kill me and set up a takeover - either by force or by controlling Liam.

What he didn't account for was the stories that they whisper about me, every single one of them fucking true.

I will bring death to Sean's door and not feel an ounce of remorse for it. Even if that means losing Avalina, as long as she lives, I don't care what happens to me.

As we make our way through the darkened streets, my senses are heightened and on alert, every sound echoing in the silence. The distant bark of a dog, the rustle of leaves in the wind, the soft crunch of our footsteps on the pavement–all of it seems amplified, the tension in the air almost tangible.

The moon slips behind the clouds, casting us into shadow. I steel myself for the battle ahead. For Avalina, I will fight against all odds, no matter the cost.

"Stay close," I instruct Liam as we approach the O'Neil manor, a grandiose show of wealth if I ever saw one. The building looms before us, with enough lights to illuminate the surrounding woods. He knows we're coming.

We know where the guards are stationed and when they change shifts, thanks to Finn, but if Sean has Avalina, he might also know his heir has been working against him, so we have to operate as if everything we know is a lie.

Heart pounding, I grip the cold steel of my gun as I tiptoe through the shadows. My eyes scan every corner, searching for any hint of movement or danger. Staying low, I crouch behind a trimmed hedge outlining the property, sensing rather than seeing the others do the same behind me.

Finn moves to take point, and as I much as I want to lead this ambush to save my girl, I know Finn has knowledge I don't. He grew up here.

Even though Sean thinks he's set up a pretty trap, even if he knows Finn has been working with me, he doesn't realize that Finn has been working against his father since he was old enough to realize that his dear old dad killed his mom.

All we have to do is make it to the east wing, to where Finn's second will let us in the house through an entrance hidden even from Sean himself.

As we turn yet another darkened corner, one that will lead us to our destination, Finn holds up a hand, signaling for us to stop. "Footsteps," he silently mouths, and my senses sharpen, listening for the telltale signs of our enemies approaching.

"Stay hidden," I whisper, before stepping out into the open, weapon raised. The moment our adversaries round the bend, their eyes widen in surprise. They never stand a chance, whether or not they know it.

"Kieran Calder," one of them spits, venom dripping from his words. "You'll regret crossing us."

"Where is she?" I demand, fury propelling my voice forward like a whip. "Tell me, or bleed out here and now."

"Go to hell!" the man sneers, defiance gleaming in his eyes.

"Very well," I reply, cold as ice. And with that, I aim and pull the trigger faster than they can, the sound like a harbinger of death. I don't allow myself to feel remorse—there is no time for such luxuries.

Chapter 30

Avalina

A shiver jolts me awake, my body stiff and cold as I struggle to make sense of the dimly lit room. Panic sets in as I realize that this is not my bedroom, and I am not alone. My heart takes off like a wild horse, pounding against my chest as I note the iron bars around me and the rope securing my hands behind my back.

Overcome by the terror rushing through my veins, my brain short circuits, my breath now coming in great, heaving gasps. Only my experience with nightmares has me automatically slowly inhaling and counting my exhales. My chest constricts and I feel like a fish on dry land, unable to breathe no matter how my lungs scream at me to do just that.

Flashes of memories slam into me of the creeps outside of the nightclub, and horror dawns, my bones shuddering in realization. They took me because of Kieran, which means I am in grave danger.

I shift against the hard, concrete floor, my short satin dress doing nothing to ward off the chill seeking into my bones. Hissing as the ropes dig into my wrists, my eyes scan the room, searching for any means of escape.

The iron bars of the cage seem to mock me, and I can't see anything past them but shadow. A single, narrow window sits high above me, taunting me with its promise of freedom. I clench my fists, feeling the desperate need to break free from this cold, suffocating place.

I know I am probably a trap or a bargaining chip for Kieran, but either way, I'm not safe, not until I get out of here and far away. Even if Kieran comes for me, which I have no doubt that he will, it doesn't mean I will live through the ordeal.

Suddenly, I can hear footsteps above me, their steady rhythm echoing through the cold, dimly lit room. Panic surges within me like a tidal wave, threatening to sweep away any semblance of resolve I'd mustered.

Scooting backwards and pressing against the wall, my heart pounds in my ears as I try to control my frantic breathing. Time is running out.

As the footsteps make their way to me, my eyes dart about the confines of my prison, searching for anything that could be used to my advantage. The only possessions I have are the clothes on my back and the small pendant Kieran had gifted me when we first met—It seems so trivial now, a mere trinket compared to the gravity of my situation.

Something glittering near the edge of the cage bars catches my attention. I do my best to silently move closer, where I find a tiny shard of glass hidden in the shadows. My heart leaps at the discovery. It isn't much, but it might just be enough. I wiggle around so my bound arms can grab the glass, shouting to hopefully cover the noise of my movement.

"Who's there?" I call out, feigning confidence as the footsteps stop. "What do you want from me?"

No response comes, only the creaking of a door as it opens. I swiftly snag the shard of glass, concealing it beneath my folded and bound hands as I prepare for whatever fate awaits me.

"Show yourself!" I demand, hoping my voice doesn't betray the quivering fear that threatens to overcome me. "I'm not afraid of you!"

"Is that so?" The voice is smooth and sinister, sending shivers down my spine. As the figure emerges from the shadows, I steel myself for what's to come.

Everything in me freezes at the sight of the older man, probably my father's age, with dark hair that seems to gleam red in the dim light. He walks towards me with a purposeful stride, a smirk ghosting his features as his large presence sucks up all the air in the room.

"Listen," I begin, trying to sound as calm and composed as possible. "I don't know who you are, or what you want with me, but I can assure you that I have nothing of value. Whatever it is you're after, I can't help you."

"Ah, but you see," the stranger replies, his voice tinged with amusement. "You're the one who's mistaken. You have something precious indeed — your life."

Fear seizes me in its claws again as the stranger takes a key out of his pocket and opens the door of the cage, grabbing me harshly by my bound arms. I can't stop the scream that crawls its way out of my throat. Terror overwhelms me as I'm dragged behind the man, stumbling to get my feet under me.

The stranger turns and backhands me, and I taste copper as blood blooms in my mouth. "No one here is going to help you," he snarls. "Shut up and do what you're told, and you may live. Fight me and I'll just kill you out of spite. Got it?"

My heart races and I nod, my voice now frozen in fear. I follow the man up a set of stairs and through a door. Once we reach the other side, light blinds me and I blink away the sting of fresh tears. My feet stop moving again as I stand in shock, feeling out of place in the luxurious home while my dress is torn, my arms are bound, and tears stream down my face.

The grip on my arm tugs me forward, past cream-colored walls with gold scones. White doors are spaced along the hallway, most of them closed. The few doors that are open give me glimpses of dark wood and damask covered chairs and couches. We make our way under a grand set of curved stairs that arch up towards a second floor, a set of wooden double doors on the other side. My guess is that they lead to the outdoors.

Glancing around, I find myself surrounded by a dozen men, all clearly armed with guns. I feel faint as I realize what is happening. The stranger with the bruising grip on my arm is Sean O'Neil, and these are the men loyal to him.

The trap, my life, it is all a way to get Kieran here. The world threatens to go black and part of me wants it to, wants to give into the darkness where I wouldn't feel this sinking in my gut and the cold wave of terror shaking my bones.

Chapter 31

KIERAN

The darkness envelops us, providing a cloak for our infiltration. Finn and I move with stealthy precision through the shadows, using every ounce of our training and experience to navigate undetected. My senses heightened, attuned to the slightest sounds as we crept further to the east wing where Finn's second was waiting.

A single thought consumed my mind: Avalina. She was the reason for every bullet loaded, every weapon held, and every life risked. And I would do whatever it took to bring her home.

My heart pounds in my chest, each beat echoing through the darkness like a war drum. As we round a corner, we spot two guards, their backs turned toward us as they whisper to each other. With silent nods, we split, each moving to take down one of the guards.

"Have you heard about the girl?" one of the guards asks, his words dripping with curiosity.

"Rumors, mostly," the other replies, a chuckle rumbling in his throat. "I hear she's quite the prize."

My blood boils at the thought of these men discussing Avalina as if she were nothing more than a trophy. Slipping behind my target, I wrap my arm around his neck, cutting off his air supply as Finn does the same to his opponent. Within moments, both guards lay unconscious on the ground.

"Nicely done," Finn grunts, admiration lacing his words. "Now let's find Avalina and get the hell out of here." He approaches a wall of the mansion and presses against something I can't see. A series of quiet knocks and the wall moves, a light from inside the house shining through the gap.

I follow Finn into the sliver of light, Cass and Liam filling in behind us. We're hunched over in a small tunnel, slowly carved away with careful precision. A set of industrial string of lights dot the wall, casting harsh shadows on the stone. I know from the stories that this tunnel leads to Finn's room, and was forged into creation during boisterous parties to hide the noise.

Finn's second, Ethan, stands before us, and even though I barely know the man, I know something was wrong by the way his jaw is tense, wanting to hold back the word that would damn his soul under the reign of my fury.

"They moved her," he mutters to Finn, blue eyes dancing in my direction. Yes, Ethan knows exactly what kind of wrath is simmering in my veins.

"To where?" I demand, stepping up into Ethan's face.

Finn doesn't even blink. He just steps in between me and Ethan, taking control and giving me a moment to choke my rage into submission once more.

"I'm not sure what he's doing. He took her out of the basement. They're all gathered in the foyer now."

"Well, fuck."

"Why? What does that mean?" Liam asks.

I know Finn can feel my eyeballs burning with rage in the back of his skull.

"He was always one for theatrics." Finn mumbles as he runs a hand through his hair.

"Finn..." I warn.

"He's not going to keep her caged. He's taking her out front, where everyone can see her. Where you can see her."

"And then what is he going to do?" Cass whispers.

"Fuck if I'm waiting here to find out," I say as I turn on my heel towards the door. I hear Liam's curse before his hand slams on my shoulder, whipping me around and against the wall. A roar begins to make its way up my throat as I move to push Liam aside when I feel the cool press of a knife against my neck.

I shift my eyes to see Cass leaning against the wall next to me with the echo of death on her face, a bigger threat than the sharp edge she holds against me. "Shut up and listen, Kieran, before you get us all killed."

I don't dare move, not with the blade pushing ever so slightly harder against my skin, a promise I knew Cass will fulfill if she felt I'm not able to rein it in, to pull the monster back by its chains into its cage.

I close my eyes and take a breath. "I'm listening."

Chapter 32

KIERAN

We take our posts around the back, lined up with the sole purpose of herding Sean and his men where we want them, out front to their cars waiting on the driveway. The only problem? Avalina is with him.

The moon hangs low in the sky, an eerie crimson glow casting long shadows across the field. My heart pounds like a drum in my chest, a drumbeat of anticipation and fear as we approach the O'Neil stronghold. I can feel Finn's presence beside me, the tense energy radiating from my friend's body.

"Ready?" Finn whispers, his breath warm against Kieran's ear. I couldn't help but admire the man's unwavering loyalty, even in the face of such danger.

"Ready," I reply, my voice barely audible. Our eyes locked, a silent communication passing between us - a shared understanding of the risks we were about to take, all for the sake of rescuing Avalina.

As one, we leap from our hiding place, weapons drawn and fierce determination etched on our faces. A surge of adrenaline washes over me, fueling every muscle, every cell, as I charge toward the unsuspecting guards.

"Surprise, you bastards!" Finn roars, his battle cry echoing through the night like a vengeful storm. The guards scramble to react, panic and confusion clouding their faces as we descend upon them like avenging angels.

Gunfire erupts around us, the deafening roar of bullets slicing through the air like demonic whispers.

"Kieran, left!" Finn shouts, his warning cutting through the cacophony of chaos. I pivot, my body moving with years of rigorous training as I dispatch another guard. Despite the progress, I can feel the weight of our mission bearing down on me, the lives we are ending in the pursuit of Avalina's safety.

As the battle rages on, my monster rears its head and I'm lost in the dance of death, each swing of my weapon a testament to the love that burns within me. I can feel the heat of Finn's body beside me, our movements synchronized like a deadly ballet.

"Move in, now!" I command, my voice steely and unwavering despite the adrenaline coursing through me. The sound of gunfire echos in the air like a symphony of violence, a cacophony that threatens to drown out all reason and sanity.

"Flank them from the left," I order Finn, my eyes never straying far from the battlefield. I can feel the familiar weight of responsibility settling on my shoulders as we fight to regain control of the situation. My friends move swiftly under my direction, their trust in me as unshakable as my resolve.

"Watch your back!" I warn Cass, gripping my weapon tightly as I prepare for the onslaught of enemy fire. Bullets whiz past us, their sharp, metallic scent filling my nostrils as they narrowly miss our bodies. The taste of fear mixed with determination coats my tongue, making it difficult to swallow.

"Move up on three!" I shout, gripping my gun tightly as I mentally prepare myself for the fight ahead. "One, two... three!"

As we surge forward, our bodies slick with sweat and determination, I can't help but think of the woman who had captured my heart, her spirit as wild and untamed as the battlefield that surrounds us.

Blood drips down my face, blurring my vision and mixing with the sweat that coats my brow. I'm not even sure where the blood is coming from.

Finn grunts in exertion as he hurls a barrage of punches at a guard, his own injuries more than clear in the blood staining his clothes.

"Kieran, we need to move!" Finn barks, his breath labored as if each word was being dragged from the depths of his lungs. "We won't last much longer!"

"Agreed," I growl, my voice hoarse from shouting orders and battle cries. "But we can't leave without Avalina."

"Trust me, I won't let that happen," he assures me, a fierce determination burning in his eyes.

"Kieran, watch your six!" Cass's voice snaps me back to reality, and I spin around just in time to take a bullet in my arm instead of my chest. Pain sears through me, hotter than any blaze, but I grit my teeth and force myself to fight through it. I can't afford to let it slow me down.

I strain with effort as I continue to engage our opponents. Every muscle screams in protest, every breath a burning ache in my chest, but surrender is not an option. Avalina's life depends on us, and I would rather die than fail her.

"Can't let them get the upper hand," Finn grunts, his voice weary with exertion, but moving still at the same, launching himself at yet another guard, taking him down with a brutal efficiency that had become second nature to him.

"Liam!" A voice screams behind me. I turn just in time to see Finn take the brunt of an attack meant for my brother. For the first time since this fight began, worry takes seed in my veins and roots me to the spot, frozen, as I watch Finn fall to the ground."

"Kieran, we're being pushed back!" Liam yells over the deafening sound of gunfire. "We need to regroup!"

"Fall back to the tree line!" I shout, grabbing Finn and pulling him with me. As we retreat, thoughts of Avalina consume me, her image flickering in my mind like a candle struggling to stay lit. I know what's at stake, but the fear of losing her fuels my every move, driving me forward even when exhaustion threatens to consume me.

"Take cover!" I call out, diving behind a fallen tree trunk just as a hail of bullets rains down upon us. My heart pounds in my chest like a wild animal trapped in a cage, desperate to escape its confines.

"Damn it," I whisper, my breath coming in ragged gasps. Our plan isn't going the way we want it to. I've got to do something fast.

Chapter 33

Sloane

I should be asleep at this hour, but I rarely sleep, preferring to use the darkness as a shield for my training. During the day, I train my mind while playing pretend, listening in on conversations through secret passages and creating new schemes to shake the tail of whatever unlucky soul was on guard duty.

When the sun gives way to the moon, that was when I shined, honing my body into lethal grace with a precision I knew even my brother couldn't beat. Sure, he was stronger. But I was faster, smarter, and didn't care about the pile of bones our lives were built on.

I had lost my humanity years ago, sacrificing it to protect my sanity in a world designed to break me.

I heard my father's men bring someone in through the basement doors a couple of hours ago, but I didn't give it too much thought. People come and go down there all the time. What do I care.

That is, until Finn texted me on my burner phone, the one I hide from everyone so I can try to have some semblance of a life. And then I heard the guards talking as they walked down the hallway, eager to take down Kieran Calder.

So here I sit, twirling my pearl-handled knife in my hands, its sides glimmering in the low light of my bedroom.

The knife matches its surroundings. White bedspread, white curtains, white rug. White as far as the eye could see. Everything white and pure and innocent for the O'Neil princess.

Even my attire is fit for the myth that swirls around me, a closet filled with dresses of all shapes and sizes, not a pair of pants in sight.

Father keeps me out of the spotlight, away from prying eyes, letting the rumors twist and choke like thorny vines. A beauty, a prize for any made man, tucked away high in her tower room of the great O'Neil manor.

A monstrosity, more like. Everything is gilded and ornate, as if that will hide the blood and bones it's built on.

And me, always guarded to keep the princess safe. But what they were really doing was trapping a monster.

I'm still swirling in my thoughts, trying to decide on the best course of action, when I hear raised voices and cheering coming from downstairs.

Leaping off my bed, I make my way to the door, looking for shadows and sounds that tell me who is on the other side. I hear nothing.

Frowning, I turn the knob silently and peer through the crack. I see nothing. Dumbfounded, I swing the door open wide, peering first down one side of the hallway and then the other. There's no one there. *What the fuck?* My door is always guarded.

Stepping back into my room, I grab my gun and quickly wrap my thigh holster on. My dress hides it well enough. Feeling nerves skate up my spine, I tuck a pocket knife into my sock nestled in my ankle boot. Something's not right. I would rather have more weapons on me, but if I'm wrong and get caught with them, I'll be in even more danger, so this will have to do for now.

I creep forward swiftly, moving like the other ghosts that haunt these halls. As I near the stairwell landing, the voices come in more clearly.

"He was spotted with Kieran on the west perimeter. My men lost sight of them, but we know they're here."

"Looks like Calder isn't the only trash we're taking out tonight," my father's voice booms. "But know this, I'll be the one to kill my son, and if any of you try to, I'll fucking kill you."

I stifle a gasp with my fist. Finn. Fuck. I may not care about much, or anything really, except for my baby brother.

My terror is interrupted as a muffled feminine voice emerges from the chaos floating up the stairs.

"I told you to shut it. Was the gag not enough of a hint to keep quiet?" my father fumes.

"Oh, I've something to keep her quiet with," another voice answers.

"All in due time. She's no use as bait if she's broken," my father says as he steps echo towards the front door, the unmistakable sounds of someone being dragged behind him.

I would know, I've been dragged before.

Keeping low, I turn back and tiptoe to my room, hoping the plan I'm hastily building in my mind doesn't fall apart and kill us all.

Chapter 34

KIERAN

Panting, I lean against the rough bark of an ancient pine at the treeline, the metallic tang of spent gunpowder still hanging heavy in the night air. Beside me, Cass's breath comes in ragged gasps, the moonlight glinting off her sweat-slicked skin. Liam crouches nearby, his normally mischievous blue eyes now scanning the dark expanse for movement, while Finn's massive form looms like a silent sentinel, his red hair a muted flame in the shadowy woods.

"Everyone alright?" My voice is a low growl, more felt than heard.

"Still kicking," Liam replies with a wry twist of his lips that doesn't reach his eyes. Cass simply nods, her chest heaving as she tries to steady her breathing.

"Good." I eye the O'Neil manor, a fortress of stone and secrets just beyond our temporary sanctuary. "We need to split up. It'll give us a better chance."

"Split up? That's your plan?" Cass's whisper is sharp with adrenaline.

"Trust me," I say, the words an unspoken command as my gaze meets hers, commanding and intense. "It's the only way."

"Alright. Let's do it," Finn says, his deep voice rumbling with the readiness for action that I've come to rely on.

"Take the front, make some noise. Be the storm they're expecting," I instruct them, my tone brooking no argument. "I'll circle around, quiet as death."

Liam claps a hand on my shoulder. "Make it count, brother."

They move out, and the forest swallows their presence, leaving me alone with the thrum of my heart and the mission at hand. I slip through the darkness, every sense heightened, moving with a predator's grace. The side of the house looms ahead, the guards unwitting pawns in a game they don't understand.

My hands are swift, my movements precise as I approach the first guard from behind. A quick chop to the carotid artery and he crumples, silenced before a cry can escape his lips. I catch him, easing his unconscious form to the ground with the care of someone handling something precious. One down, more to go.

The second guard isn't as lucky. His mistake is turning at the last moment, eyes widening in terror. There's no time for subtlety now. My fist connects with his jaw, a crack echoing in the cool air, and he goes down hard. I drag his limp body into the underbrush, a prayer for forgiveness whispered into the night.

With the path clear, I find myself at the window, its pane reflecting a distorted version of myself back at me. For a moment, I see not a man but a specter, a ghost of vengeance and unspoken desires. Then I push those thoughts aside. This isn't the time for reflection—it's the time for action.

My elbow, wrapped in the thick fabric of my jacket, makes quick work of the glass. It shatters with a satisfying crash, shards falling like raindrops of rebellion. I'm through the window in an instant, the familiar smell of old books and whisky greeting me as I step into the lion's den. The O'Neil manor, with all its shadows and sins, now houses a new secret—me.

The study is a sanctuary of solitude, a rich tapestry of knowledge and power woven into every book-laden shelf and polished mahogany surface. I move with silent purpose, the ghost of my reflection haunting the glass doors of antique cabinets. My fingers trail across the spines of leather-bound tomes, brushing against the accumulated wisdom of generations that will soon be lost to the flames.

Beneath the heavy, somber portrait of some long-dead patriarch, I find my weapon of choice—not a blade or a bullet, but a crystal decanter of aged scotch. It glints seductively in the dim light, promising oblivion. I consider a sip, a brief respite for my parched throat, but there's no time for the indulgence of vices, not when vengeance courses through my veins like a wild, raging river.

I uncap the decanter with a swift, calculated motion, the scent of peat and wood smoke permeating the air, intoxicating in its potency. The curtains beckon me, opulent velvet that has never felt the caress of anything less than golden sunlight. They'll burn beautifully. I tilt the decanter, and the liquid cascades out, each droplet catching the moonlight as it races to soak the fabric. It's almost a shame, this desecration of finery, but the thought is fleeting, smothered by the roar of blood in my ears.

The alcohol snakes its way across the Persian rug, an expensive piece now marred by my deliberate vandalism. The desk, littered with papers that whisper secrets of wealth and corruption, receives the same dousing, the liquid greedily absorbed by parchments filled with deceit.

Finally, I stand back, the decanter empty, its purpose served. The air is thick with the fumes of impending destruction, an acrid prelude to the symphony of chaos I am about to conduct. From my pocket, I retrieve the lighter, a simple instrument of silver that gleams with deadly promise. My thumb rolls over the flint wheel, a spark of life birthing a small, dancing flame.

With a flick of my wrist, the fire leaps from the lighter to the soaked curtain, a passionate kiss igniting an inferno. The heavy fabric, once a symbol of his ill-gotten wealth, soaks up the fuel eagerly. I can't help but feel a sense of grim satisfaction. This is more than just a fire; it's retribution. With a flick of the lighter, flames dance to life, hungry and relentless. My heart beats a furious rhythm, echoing the crackle and roar that begins to consume the room.

"Time to go," I whisper to myself, backing out into the hallway. The heat licks at my back, a beast unleashed, tearing through the gaudy interior of Sean's fortress.

As I move back out the window I broke through, the sound of alarms and the clamor of disoriented voices reach me. Sean's guards are shouting orders, their focus shifting from guarding to salvaging. They scramble, tripping over themselves in a desperate attempt to contain the blaze that's eating up the mansion's innards.

The night air is cool against my sweat-drenched skin. I sprint across the lawn, senses on high alert. My gaze locks onto the front where Sean stands, his figure illuminated by the eerie glow of the inferno behind me.

There she is. Avalina. Her shoulder-length copper hair reflecting the light of the fire, outlining her like a vengeful angel. She's on her knees, and I can see even from this distance, the defiance in her green eyes. It's that same spirit that drew me to her, long before the accident that stole her memories of us. Blood is splattered across her face and dripping down her torn dress, her wide eyes meeting mind across the expanse between us.

"Kieran, we've got three coming your way," Liam warns, his voice cool but strained on my earpiece, signaling the effort he's putting into taking down Sean's men.

"Thanks," I respond, not breaking stride as Cass, silent as a shadow, emerges from the bushes to my left. Her movements are graceful and lethal.

"Go, I've got these," she whispers, her eyes glinting with the thrill of the fight.

"Thanks, Cass," I say, sparing her a brief nod before continuing my advance.

My heart hammers against my ribcage, each beat a drum of war as I approach my nemesis. Sean's eyes meet mine, a smirk on his lips, but I see it—the flicker of fear. He knows what I am capable of. He knows this night won't end well for him.

"Come and get her, Kieran," he taunts, voice cutting through the chaos. But I'm already moving, already planning the moment I reclaim what he has stolen from me.

Avalina's safety is all that matters now. Everything else—the fire, the family feud, the past—it all fades away. There's only her, and the burning need to pull her from the clutches of a madman. I'm close now, so close, and I can almost feel the warmth of her skin, the pulse of her life beneath my fingertips.

Sean's hand is tangled in her chestnut hair, the barrel of his gun cold against her temple.

"Kieran," she whispers, her voice trembling through the veil of smoke and fear.

"Let her go, Sean," I growl, the words tearing from my throat like shards of glass.

Sean sneers, tightening his grip on Avalina. "Drop your weapon and get on your knees, or she dies."

Every muscle in my body screams to charge forward, to unleash the fury boiling within me, but Avalina's life hangs by a thread—a thread Sean would sever without a second thought. With a snarl of defeat, I let my gun clatter to the ground and slowly sink to my knees.

"Good boy," he mocks, his laughter grating against my ears. "But here's the twist, Kieran. You think you'll watch her die? No. She'll watch you die."

I can feel Avalina's gaze on me, filled with a silent plea. The air thickens with the scent of fire and blood, and I brace for the moment Sean will pull the trigger.

But Avalina is not just a helpless damsel. In a sudden blur of motion, she shatters the stillness, driving a shard of glass deep into Sean's leg. His howl pierces the night, and the gun spins away from her head as he turns on her with venomous fury.

"Stupid girl!" he roars, fingers clawing to pull the trigger.

Then, a shot rings out—not from Sean's gun but from above, where smoke billows around the shadowy figure of Sloane. The firearm explodes from Sean's grasp, skittering across the lawn, leaving him weaponless and writhing.

"Run, Avalina!" I shout, my heart hammering with adrenaline and hope.

For a moment, time stands still—the flames' dance, the distant cries of combat, even the stench of betrayal—all fade into the background as Avalina scrambles toward me, her survival instinct taking over.

"Kieran," she breathes, her hands reaching for mine.

"Go," I urge, my voice laced with both command and concern, as I shove her away from the fire and carnage, towards where I see Cass against the treeline.

The world slows to a crawl as I lunge toward the earth, fingers scrabbling against the cool grass, desperately seeking my discarded weapon. It's a lifeline—my only chance to end this madness once and for all. The metallic coldness of the gun handle presses into my palm, and it's like a jolt of electricity through my veins, a spark of hope in the engulfing darkness.

But Sean is a shadow slipping away, his figure blurry through the haze of smoke and flames. He stumbles toward the sleek black car parked haphazardly on the driveway. My breath catches as he dives inside, engine roaring to life, tires screeching against the gravel with a sense of urgency that matches the pounding of my heart.

My gaze follows the taillights disappearing into the night, a red beacon of the endgame. There's a part of me that wants to chase, to hunt him down like the predator I am. But I know Sean's time is quickly running out.

Sean's car hits a sharp turn, but because of the brake lines I cut a few hours ago, he can't slow down. It's a violent ballet of metal and momentum as the vehicle flips, once, twice—time seems to stretch, dragging out the moment into an eternity until, with a sound like the world itself splitting open, it explodes. Fire blooms against the night sky, a deadly flower of retribution, and with it, the last remnants of Sean O'Neil vanish into nothingness.

For a heartbeat, there's silence—a void where even the crackling flames dare not whisper. Then reality rushes back in like a tidal wave, and with it comes the clamor of surrender. Sean's men drop their weapons, hands raised, their spirits broken by the spectacle of their leader's downfall.

"Kieran!" Avalina's cry is raw, desperate.

Our eyes lock across the smoldering battlefield, twin storms of emotion colliding in a single glance. Her green eyes are oceans of turmoil, but beneath the fear and the shock, there's something else—relief, love, a connection that burns brighter than any flame.

We run to each other, heedless of the danger, the debris, the world falling apart around us. The distance closes, each step pounding a rhythm of longing into the earth until, finally, we collide. Her arms wrap around me, fierce and unyielding, and I pull her close, burying my face in the softness of her hair. Our lips meet in a kiss that is both a promise and a prayer.

"Kieran," she whispers against my mouth, and the sound is more intoxicating than any liquor, any drug. "You're here."

A shuddering sigh rolls out of me, and I clutch her tight to my chest, my chin resting on the top of her head.

"Never again," I whisper, my voice raw with emotion. "I'm never walking away from you again."

Chapter 35

Avalina

I gaze out at the hospital window, eyes cast to the light fading over the horizon, the setting sun making the city glow.

I haven't been awake long, and I need more sleep, but my mind keeps replaying the events of the past couple of days over and over, a loop I can't escape. My chest tightens at the memory of Sean and the gun pressed against me, fear leaving a cold trail down my spine that has my breaths coming in soft gasps.

The sound of a blanket moving has me turning to see a tousled Kieran sit up in the chair next to me, running a hand through his hair.

"Kieran," I whisper, my voice barely audible above the sound of my own ragged breaths as he moves to sit next to me on the hospital bed. I look into his eyes, torn between the love that swells within me and the knowledge of the darkness that lurks in his life.

Before me is the man who had captivated me with his charm, his intellect, and his undeniable passion. But beneath that tantalizing façade, I now understand the truth of the sinister world he inhabits. The truth of why he tried to push me away.

"Lina, are you—" he begins, but I hold up a hand to silence him.

"Please, don't say anything just yet." My fingers tremble as my mind tries to spin a web with my conflicting emotions, putting the pieces together of everything I have learned. Some pieces are sharp with jagged edges and looking at them too long makes my heart bleed.

I am pulled to Kieran like the moon to the earth. Even with most of our relationship in memories locked away, I can't escape his orbit, a force so powerful it threatens to consume me entirely.

But even with that magnetic pull of my connection to Kieran, I realize I can no longer turn a blind eye to the sins committed by those whose blood runs through his veins.

Kieran's gaze bares into mine, seeking any sign of forgiveness or understanding, but all he finds is a storm of emotion swirling in the depths of my emerald eyes. In that moment, I wish I can erase everything I have learned about this town and all the dark deeds that run beneath the surface.

The door to my room opens and Iris walks in, her eyes wide once she spots me. "You're awake!"

At her exclamation, a commotion echoes in the hallway, with Claire and Amanda quickly following Iris into the room.

"Oh, Avie!" Claire exclaims, "I was so worried about you! I didn't know what to do when you disappeared at the club."

Iris interrupts. "Claire called me, and I called Kieran. I knew if anyone could help, it was him."

I blink at this statement, so unlike how Iris talked about Kieran the last time we discussed it.

Iris grabs my hands in hers. "I know what you're thinking, Avie. I was wrong. If it wasn't for Kieran, who knows if you'd even be alive right now. He saved you."

I see Kieran frown over Claire's shoulder, and he speaks the words I know he's thinking. "No, I was the one that put Avalina in danger. If she was never in a relationship with me, Sean wouldn't have targeted her."

Iris whips around and smacks Kieran on the shoulder. "No, you don't get to say things like that. Sean made his choices because he was a horrible person. You made choices because you love Avalina."

Kieran's eyes soften at that. "You're right, I do love her," he says as his eyes meet mine.

As our gazes lock, unspoken promises and fears tangle together like the threads of a tapestry, weaving an uncertain path forward.

I turn my gaze back to Iris, who is patting my hand. It is clear that the two have been talking while I was asleep. "How long was I out?"

"Almost a day."

Claire walks to the other side of the bed, sitting next to me. "I'm so sorry, Avie, I should have gone with you outside. I shouldn't have left you alone."

I clutch Claire's hand. "No, no, it's not your fault. Iris is right. The only person who is at fault is Sean O'Neil."

Kieran clears his throat and Iris and Claire exchange a look I can't decipher before my friends make excuses to clear the room.

It feels like stones are gathering in my chest, weighing me down and rooting me to the spot, caught in Kieran's snare.

"Kieran," I begin, my voice wavering, "Is everything okay? Are we safe now?"

"Yes, we're safe, Lina." Kieran says, placing a kiss on the top of my head. "Sean and those loyal to him are gone."

"What about Finn?"

"He's fine. The doctor says it will take some time for him to recover, so Slone has stepped in for now. She seems to have a firm hand on things."

"That doesn't surprise me, given how she risked her life to save me. To save us."

"Lina, I want you to know. It's all over now. You're safe now. I promise. No matter what you want to do with your life, where you want to go, who you want to be with."

"Who I want to *be* with?" I can't keep the sharp bite out of my tone. "Do I have a choice now?"

"I fucked up. I thought staying away would protect you, but I just put you in more danger. I'm so sorry, Avalina."

"Sorry doesn't make up for the new nightmares, Kieran." Anger surges, hot and molten. My words flow like an angry torrent that seeks every chink in Kieran's armor. "You walked away."

Kieran flinches but holds my gaze all the same, willing to take every blow I can give.

"I know, and I'll spend the rest of my life making it up to you, if you let me."

My rage cools at the unwavering oath Kieran is offering. But I'm still unsure if I want to accept.

Kieran's world holds a savage violence that most would run from, afraid of the beasts that lurk in the night. But I understand games of power, and I trust Kieran is one of the few that seeks the crown not to control, but to protect.

The question is, did I trust that Kieran can protect me? If I stay by his side, if I stay in his life, will there be another repeat of the nightmare currently replaying in my mind?

I feel the warmth of Kieran's breath on my skin, like a flame dancing dangerously close to kindling.

"Kieran," I say, my voice wavering, "I–" But the words halt in my throat, choked by the storm within me. I want to trust him, to accept his promise and let our love guide us through the shadows. But the weight of this town's darkness bares down on me, suffocating the very air around us.

Our love is an ember that burns brightly in the darkness, but it will take more than just passion to banish the shadows forever.

The dimly lit room seems to shrink, as if the walls are closing in on us. Kieran's nervousness is palpable, etching across every line of his face and echoing in the tremor of his hands. His gaze, full of remorse and desperation, pierces my heart like a searing arrow.

"Lina," Kieran whispers, his voice cracking with emotion, "I never wanted this life. Before your accident, we talked about walking away, both of us. Away from this town, this life. I know things haven't gone the way either of us wants, but we don't have to be defined by our experiences. We can start together, you and I. Make our own choices."

My breath hitches as I study his earnest expression. His raw vulnerability tugs at my heart, making it difficult to tear my eyes from his soulful depths.

"Kieran..." I hesitate, the weight of my decision looming like an unyielding force.

"Can you really escape your family's darkness? Or will it continue to haunt us?" My words hang in the air, heavy with doubt. My heart aches at the thought of a future filled with shadows and secrets, even as my love for him roars like wildfire within my chest.

"I would follow you through the depths of hell, Lina. To another realm entirely. Nothing else matters but you. Your safety. Your happiness. You are my light, and I will go where you lead."

The sincerity in his words wound around my heart like a silken thread, drawing me closer to him, despite the storm of doubt that raged within me. I know I can never fully forget the darkness that has been revealed with Sean's actions, but as I look into Kieran's eyes, I yearn to believe in the possibility of redemption.

For a moment, the room seems to hold its breath, the silence thick and heavy with anticipation. Then, Kieran closes the distance between us, his powerful arms enveloping me in an embrace that is equal parts desperation and relief. Our bodies press together, molding to one another as if they were two halves of a whole seeking solace in each other's presence.

"Kiss me, Lina," Kieran whispers against my ear, his voice low and urgent. "Kiss me like you mean it, like you believe in us."

And though I know that the path ahead is uncertain, I can't deny the fire that burns within me as Kieran kisses me—a fire that promises to illuminate even the darkest corners of our hearts. It is this fire, this passion, that fuels my resolve and gives me the strength to face whatever challenges are ahead. For in Kieran's arms, there is a love that transcends darkness, a love that can burn bright enough to chase away the night.

Epilogue

KIERAN

Grabbing the ivory cotton tote bag from the passenger seat, I get out of my car, trying to shake off the nerves that had my heartbeat pounding in my ears. I was Kieran Calder. I didn't get anxious. But here I was, sweaty palms swiping through my hair, the jet strands now falling into my eyes instead of being artfully brushed away from my face. I winced as I slammed the car door a little too forcefully. I didn't know what to do with myself. Everything felt too big and too much. *What the fuck was wrong with me?*

Cursing, I stomped my way to Lina's apartment, shaking my head at my idiocy. It was just jewelry. A piece of metal. Like a gun. I could do this.

Knocking on Lina's door, I took a deep breath that froze in my lungs as it swung inward to reveal Avalina's smiling face.

"Come in, dinner's ready," she quipped, not realizing how tightly my muscles were strung, quivering under my skin.

I walked in behind her, a cautious predator wary of the shadows. Conan ran up to me and I bent down to scoop him up in my arms, rubbing him behind the ears the way he liked. Avalina was back in the kitchen, stirring the creamy shrimp bisque, which smelled amazing. Conan swatted at the bag still in my arms, so I put him down and began unloading my haul onto the kitchen bar.

"Fresh bread and dessert, as requested."

Lina turns, immediately grabbing the bread and inhaling. I do my best to hide the laugh that wants to race past my lips, but there is no fooling her.

Her eyes narrow at me. "What? I love bread, okay?"

Holding my hands up in mock surrender, I nod. "As one should."

She huffs as she places the bread in the oven to keep it warm before turning back to my parcels. "Kieran, you didn't have to bring an entire cake! And champagne? Why did you bring champagne?"

Shrugging, I take both from her, placing the cake out of Conan's reach and putting the champagne on ice. "I thought it would be nice to celebrate," I say, taking both from her, placing the cake out of Conan's reach, and putting the champagne on ice. "It's been months since the shooting and everything seems to be calm now. We're all in a good place." I realize I'm rambling and clear my throat, glancing at Lina, who seems absorbed in her cooking.

Deciding that changing the subject is the best course of action, I steer the ship in another direction. "How was work at the library today?"

Lina takes two pretty blue bowls down from the cabinet, so I grab some spoons and glasses, filing them with water before placing them on the bar counter.

"It was good," she says as she ladles the bisque into the bowls and grabs the steaming bread from the oven. "The new book club is really growing and our partnership program is coming along nicely."

"Nice. You should be proud of all the hard work you put into that program."

She smiles up at me as we sit down next to each other. "I am. It's really exciting to see it all come together," she says as she reaches to grab some bread and break it into small pieces. "How are things at the art gallery?"

"Good. Claire has been showing me the ropes. I'm catching on to things quickly."

Lina hums in acknowledgement as she sips on a spoonful of bisque, nodding. "I thought you would. You have a good eye for it."

I motion to the soup. "This is great, Lina."

"Thanks, I got the recipe from Iris. I think I may like the bread more, though."

I can't stop the laugh that rumbles in my chest at that. "Don't worry, I can always get you more."

"I'm going to hold you to that."

We continue to eat, talking about work and books, when a demanding yowl interrupted my thoughts. I looked down to see furry brown paws coming to rest on the side of my leg. "No, Conan, put your weapons away," I scoff as I move the cat away from me before he can dig his claws in. It wouldn't be the first time he's done it. I can't help but smile at him, even if he isn't above violence to get some food.

As Lina gathers our dishes and takes them to the sink, I grab the champagne and cake, placing them on the table with new plates and forks. I blink as I fight the urge to wipe my suddenly very sweaty palms on my pants. Doubts race through my mind as Conan weaves between my legs, probably hoping I'll give him some cake. I knew I had a choice here. I could keep going on the path I planned for tonight or I could take a detour. There was no rush, no expectation. I knew all of this. *So why was I panicking?*

Taking a deep breath, I walked over to the large window in the living room that was currently filling the space with the shimmering golden hues of sunset. The sounds of running water and bowls clinking in the dishwasher faded as I looked out at the city, awash in the dimming light of day. I was kidding anyone. I knew exactly why I was panicking. During the past months, I had let Lina see all of me.

She knew all of my secrets. The people I had killed. How much I had enjoyed it. How some days I had fucking craved it.

And she didn't run away in a panic, calling me a monster. She didn't understand, but yet she did. We grew up in different cages, and developed different ways of coping, but she knew what it was to crave an escape, to feel anything to remind yourself that you were still alive. Being with Lina, being seen by her, it kept my monster content. I hadn't felt the need to exact revenge since the night Sean O'Neil died.

So here I was, toying with a ring in my pocket and panicking that despite all of our history, despite everything we had been through together, in the end, I wouldn't be enough.

I was so lost in thought that I almost jumped as Lina came up behind me and wrapped her arms around my waist, hugging me from behind.

"You seem lost in thought. Everything okay?"

"Yeah," I cover her hands with my own, the scars scattered across my knuckles shining silver in the sunlight. "Just thinking."

"About what?" she says as she nuzzles against me, her soothing scent of jasmine and sandalwood surrounding me.

"Us," I say as I turn towards her, her hands still grasped in my own. Bending down to one knee, I lay my heart at her feet, willing to take whatever she will give it. "Lina, I love you. There is no one else for me, there never has been. It's you. Only you. And I know we come from different worlds, but I..."

"Kieran, stop."

I look up, frozen in place with fear as one of Lina's hands unravels from my grasp to rest on my cheek. My heart begins a staccato rhythm in my chest and my monster opens a sleepy eye as the commotion.

"Yes, Kieran. Yes," Avalina whispers as tears slide down her face.

Releasing a shuddering exhale, I stand as clutch Lina's face. "Yes? You mean?"

"Yes, I'll marry you," she laughs through her tears.

"You haven't even seen the ring yet..." I drift off.

Her laugh becomes louder now. "I don't care about the ring," she chuckles as she leans towards me and I meet her halfway, abandoning my fear as her lips meet mine and my monster goes back to sleep, huffing in annoyance that my stupidity woke him up.

Avalina pulls away and her green eyes bore into mine. "I only want you."

Made in the USA
Middletown, DE
06 May 2024

53907185R00215